Night Scare

Frank glanced in the rearview mirror for the third or fourth time in the past few moments.

"What's up?" Joe asked.

"I'm not sure," Frank said. "The same car's been right behind us for a long time." Frank took a series of quick right turns, leaving and then circling back to their normal route home.

"Still there?" Joe asked.

"Nope. I'm just paranoid, I guess."

The Hardys came to their street, and Frank started slowing for their driveway. Up ahead, a set of headlights winked on, piercing the darkness. The lights came closer, then angled toward the van. White light filled the windshield.

"What's that car doing?" Joe asked.

Frank slammed on the brakes. "Hold on!" he shouted. "It's coming straight for us!"

The Hardy Boys Mystery Stories

Available from MINSTREL Books

161

TRAINING FOR TROUBLE

FRANKLIN W. DIXON

A MINSTREL® BOOK

Published by POCKET BOOKS
New York   London   Toronto   Sydney   Singapore

This book is a work of fiction. Names, characters, places and incidents are products of the author's imagination or are used fictitiously. Any resemblance to actual events or locales or persons, living or dead, is entirely coincidental.

A MINSTREL PAPERBACK *Original*

A Minstrel Book published by
POCKET BOOKS, a division of Simon & Schuster Inc.
1230 Avenue of the Americas, New York, NY 10020

Copyright © 2000 by Simon & Schuster Inc.

Front cover illustration by Jeff Walker

All rights reserved, including the right to reproduce
this book or portions thereof in any form whatsoever.
For information address Pocket Books, 1230 Avenue
of the Americas, New York, NY 10020

ISBN: 0-671-04758-2

First Minstrel Books printing May 2000

10 9 8 7 6 5 4 3 2 1

THE HARDY BOYS MYSTERY STORIES is a trademark
of Simon & Schuster Inc.

THE HARDY BOYS, A MINSTREL BOOK and colophon
are registered trademarks of Simon & Schuster Inc.

Printed in the U.S.A.

Contents

TRAINING FOR TROUBLE

1 Shocking Touch

Joe Hardy crouched low and flexed his left hand. Somehow he had jammed his wrist during the last skirmish. Shaking off the pain, he circled to his left. His opponent was quick and strong, and Joe had to be ready to defend himself.

"What now?" he asked.

"Don't let him get an inside grip," someone shouted.

"Keep your feet apart," another voice added.

Before Joe could sort out the advice, his opponent was on him again, grabbing for his collar.

The two of them locked together, each clutching fistfuls of the other's shirt. Their heads knocked together, and Joe felt a splash of sweat or blood trickle down his brow. He shifted his balance, trying to catch his opponent off guard, but the guy anticipated his every move.

It was Friday evening, and Joe, his brother, Frank, and a few hundred other citizens of Bayport had been invited to tour the new Olympic Combat-Sports Training Facility.

Here, athletes from the U.S. Olympic and Junior Olympic fencing, archery, judo, and biathlon teams would train year-round for their events. While most of the visitors were milling around the equipment or taking a tour of the building, some brave souls, like Joe, were allowed to test their skills against the best athletes in the world.

Joe took a couple of deep breaths. He'd held his own during his judo match until that last fall, when he had been caught in a painful arm lock. He had managed to rip free by turning a somersault to untwist his arm and was about to counter when Reid Sokal, head coach of the Junior Olympic teams stepped in and said not to fight too hard. He was afraid someone might get seriously hurt.

Now they were facing off for the final fall, with neither one willing to let up on the intensity.

Joe's opponent shuffled his feet, and Joe saw his chance. He yanked back hard, then quickly stepped forward, placing his left foot behind the other guy to sweep his legs out from under him. He pushed with all his might.

Joe felt his opponent's grip on his collar relax. For a split second he had a feeling of triumph—he was about to toss an experienced black belt to the floor with a perfectly executed inner reaping throw!

Somehow, that didn't happen.

Joe found himself falling forward. He fought to keep his balance, but a sharp blow to his stomach made him gasp and lifted him off his feet. He reached for something to hold on to—but caught only air. The floor, then the ceiling, rotated by in what seemed like slow motion.

His brain was still trying to figure out what went wrong when he landed on his back with a rib-rattling *whump!*

Joe lay still. He looked up at the ceiling and watched the fans high above turn slowly. He smelled the new rubber of the judo mat beneath him. But he couldn't hear anything. His ears seemed stopped up, plugged.

Then, all at once, voices broke through.

"Nice throw, Allen!" someone shouted.

"Beautiful countermove, man!"

A stocky guy with dark hair trimmed in a military-style crew cut appeared above Joe, his hand extended to help him up. It was Allen Frierson, the opponent who'd just nailed him with a nifty throw.

Joe grabbed Allen's hand and hoisted himself to his feet.

"Good match," he said, slapping Allen on the back. "But what happened?"

Frank Hardy stepped onto the mat. "You got tossed through the air like a rag doll," he told his younger brother with a grin.

Joe rubbed his wrist. "Why don't *you* go a couple of falls, smart guy? See how long you last."

Frank smiled. "No way. Being treated like a crash-test dummy isn't my idea of a good time."

Frank Hardy was one year older than his brother and, at six-one, an inch taller. Though he was just as good an athlete as Joe, he liked to make use of his quickness and skill rather than brute strength.

Allen Frierson introduced himself to Frank. "That was a stomach throw I used on your brother," he said.

"It happened too fast," Joe said.

Allen nodded. "When you pushed forward at me, I dropped to the ground. Instead of pulling you on top of me, I jammed my foot into your stomach and flipped you back over my head."

"Pretty effective," Frank said.

"Good job, kid. You have fun?" Coach Sokal asked, striding onto the mat and tossing a towel to Joe.

Joe smiled and draped the towel over his blond

4

hair like a hood. "Yeah, but I think I'll stick to football for now."

Sokal laughed, but his expression changed as he turned to Allen. "You need to be more aggressive if you want to make my team, Frierson," he said. "Stop waiting around for something to happen."

Coach Sokal appeared to be in his midthirties, and to Joe he resembled a super-tough army sergeant. His hands were oversized, and his ears were rubbery and scarred from hundreds of falls.

He wore jeans and a gray sweatshirt emblazoned with the training facility logo: an American flag with two pairs of small figures in silhouette facing off in judo and fencing while others posed with an archery bow and a target rifle.

"Stick around," Sokal said, turning back to Joe. "You'll get to watch Allen here get the same treatment you got."

"What do you mean?" Joe asked.

"We're putting on an exhibition," Coach Sokal said. He slapped Frierson on the shoulder with his clipboard. "Allen and Jake Targan are going to demonstrate some moves for the crowd. Allen, you're prey."

Sokal turned and walked purposefully over to the next mat, where one girl was showing another how to do a one-arm shoulder throw.

Frank saw that Allen's calm expression had turned into a scowl. "What's up?" he asked Allen.

"It's my turn to be the crash-test dummy," Allen replied. "Jake Targan is the top junior fighter in the country, and he just happens to be in my weight class."

"But he's been practicing a lot longer than you have, right?" Joe said.

"That's true," Allen said, nodding. "He's been a black belt since he was ten. I wrestled in high school and started judo just a couple of years ago."

"So give yourself a break," Frank said. "You'll whip up on Targan soon enough."

"Not fast enough for some people," Allen said, glancing toward the scorer's table where a tall, balding man in a crewneck sweater stood talking to the team trainer.

"Who's that?" Joe asked.

"My dad," Frierson said. "He's an electrician, but that isn't good enough for me, I guess."

"He pushes you pretty hard?" Joe asked.

"Worse than Coach Sokal," Allen replied. "His dream is to see me on the gold-medal podium at the Olympics in four years. According to him, Jake Targan is my mortal enemy."

As the teens talked, the door to the men's locker room was opened and a young man wearing a judo suit with a towel draped over his shoulders stepped out onto the crowded floor.

"He doesn't look much like a judo expert," Frank noted.

Joe agreed. Targan appeared mild and relaxed, as if he were entering a party with all his best friends. He was tall, at around six feet, but not heavily muscled. Short, curly brown hair and smooth cheeks that still held some baby fat made him appear to be about thirteen or fourteen years old.

"He's stronger than he looks," Allen said.

"Yeah, you can tell by the way he walks," Frank agreed.

Targan moved through the crowd easily, his balance shifting almost imperceptibly from one bare foot to the other as he stepped around and between people and made his way to the mats.

Targan introduced himself to the Hardys and knocked fists with Frierson. "You want to be predator or prey?" he asked.

"Coach says I'm prey," Allen replied.

"That's tough," Targan said, tightening his black belt around his waist.

"Predator or prey?" Frank asked.

"In an exhibition, one person demonstrates all the holds and falls," Targan said.

"And the other person just lets himself get flipped

around like a human bean bag," Frierson added. "That's me, as usual."

"All right, everybody!" Coach Sokal's voice boomed over the intercom system. The Hardys turned and saw him standing next to the judges' table with a microphone in his hand.

"It's eight o'clock," he said. "Gather around the mat here for a demonstration of one of the oldest fighting arts. In Japanese, *judo* means 'the gentle way,' but you'll see that competitive judo really isn't gentle at all."

The Hardys stepped off the mat to give the two combatants room. From the sidelines they watched as Sokal put the microphone down and not so gently pushed a few visitors to the side as he disappeared into the crowd.

"Check it out," Joe said as the Hardys watched Sokal break through a line of people with a television news crew in tow. The Hardys recognized the reporter leading the crew as Rachel Baden.

"Sokal's got the cameraman by the arm," Frank said. "He's practically forcing him to cover the exhibition."

A woman in a dark-red pants suit knifed through the crowd and met Sokal face-to-face, her finger pointing at his chest.

"Whoa! I want to hear this," Joe said. He and his brother edged their way between the mat and the crowd, getting close enough to hear what appeared to be a serious conversation.

The woman, her dark hair swinging across her shoulders, turned to Rachel Baden, the reporter. "I thought you were going to interview members of the fencing team. I set it all up," she said quietly.

"I think we'll have time to get over there, Ms. Montreux," Baden replied.

"Let them get a couple of falls, Geneve," Sokal said to the woman in the pants suit. He motioned for Allen and Jake to come over to him. "Come on! You got to admit judo'll make better TV than fencing."

"The woman in the red pants suit must be the director of the facility," Frank said. "Geneve Montreux."

"We agreed on a schedule—" Montreux began but stopped when she noticed the cameraman focusing on her. She obviously didn't want to make a scene.

"I'll tell the fencers they'll have to wait to be interviewed," she said, then stepped back into the crowd.

Once she was gone, Sokal walked back and picked up the microphone to introduce Jake and Allen to the crowd. "We have two talented young men to show you the basics of this ancient fighting art," Sokal said. "Jake Targan is captain of the Junior Olympic team and a two-time National Junior Champion. And Allen Frierson is one of the determined young people training here to try to make the team."

Joe saw Mr. Frierson wince as he heard his son's modest introduction.

The Hardys watched Coach Sokal describe different judo throws before Targan executed them on Frierson.

"If you're shorter than your opponent, the shoulder wheel can be a devastating move," Sokal said.

Targan and Frierson faced off for a second, then Targan ducked in low, pulling Frierson over his shoulders in what looked like a fireman's carry.

Instead of stopping with Allen safely draped over his shoulders, Targan continued lifting and pulling. Frierson's legs flew in the air as Targan flipped him onto the mat like a butcher slamming a side of beef onto a counter.

"Oh, man," Joe said. "That had to hurt."

"Yeah, I don't want to watch," Frank said. "Let's go see what the girls are up to."

Frank and Joe made their way through the crowd toward the fencing area at the far end of the gym. As they walked, they heard the crowd around the judo mat gasp. "Allen must've taken another bad fall," Joe said.

Tall, multipaned windows lined the long back wall of the gym. Three long, narrow tracks the shape of bowling lanes jutted out from the wall. Each track had a small table next to it, centered. On each table were two red lights.

Joe's girlfriend, Iola Morton, came jogging up to the Hardys. She was wearing a white fencing jacket and a vest made of metallic mesh. Her fencing mask was pushed back, and her gray eyes shone with excitement.

"On guard!" she said, stopping in front of Joe and pointing a foil at his chest.

"Hey, careful!" Joe said, backing away.

"Relax, silly," Iola said. She ran her thumb up the flexible blade of the sword to the tip. "See, the end is pretty blunt. You'd have to hit somebody just right to break the skin. But now we're going to have a real fencing match."

Frank spotted a person with a fencing mask and blond hair sticking out from under her mask. He figured it had to be his girlfriend, Callie Shaw, and waved. She held her foil in front of her mask and moved it out from her face toward him in a formal bow.

Frank laughed. "Get Iola, Callie," he shouted as Callie went back to practicing parries, thrusts, and lunges.

One of the assistant coaches called Iola over as the Hardys sat down in folding chairs next to the fencing strip.

The assistant coach made Iola stand still while she pulled a cord from the back of her metallic vest and plugged a long wire into it.

"What's she doing?" Joe asked.

"Hooking the girls up to the scoring light," Frank

11

replied. "When the tip of your foil hits your opponent's metal vest, it completes an electrical circuit."

"And makes one of the lights come on," Joe said.

"Right. It's called scoring a touch. They need the lights because things happen so fast in fencing."

After the coach had both girls hooked up to the lights, she directed them to their on-guard lines and told them to stand ready.

Iola and Callie faced each other across the center line, their foils held ready.

The next few seconds went by so quickly, Frank and Joe had trouble realizing what happened.

The coach ordered the two girls to fence. Iola and Callie stepped toward each other at the same time.

Frank saw Callie score a touch at the same time that there was a loud *pop!* Sparks shot from the tip of Callie's weapon and Iola flew backward as if she'd been shot.

2 Human Bull's-Eye

Joe jumped up from his chair. "Iola!" he shouted.

Iola lay motionless, her foil rolling idly away from her. Callie stood frozen in shock.

A fencer from the next strip whipped off her mask and rushed to Iola's side. The Hardys were there a split-second later.

As Joe and the other fencer gently removed Iola's mask, Geneve Montreux came running over, followed by the news crew and a few members of the crowd.

"Victoria, what happened?" Montreux asked.

"I don't know," the young woman at Iola's side answered. "Something with the scoring wires, I think."

Montreux knelt beside the Hardys. Joe lifted Iola's

13

head, and her eyes fluttered open as if she were waking from a deep sleep. "My shoulder," she said, reaching over with her good hand.

"Oh, no!" Montreux gasped. "I'm so sorry you got hurt, honey."

Joe ripped at the sleeve of Iola's fencing jacket. A rude red welt the size of a half dollar blistered Iola's shoulder.

"That's a nasty burn," Joe said.

"Are you okay?" Montreux asked. "How do you feel?"

"A little shaky," Iola said, sitting up. "I think I can stand."

"She must've gotten a shock from the tip of Callie's foil," Frank said.

Montreux sent someone to get one of the athletic trainers, then stood to face the gathering crowd. "Everything's okay," she said, waving them back. "We had a minor accident, but it's okay now."

Rachel Baden stuck her microphone in Montreux's face. "What happened?"

"We're not sure," Montreux stated. "We have new equipment that may have been set up incorrectly."

Montreux, with the help of Coach Sokal, answered more questions while Joe, Frank, and Callie took care of Iola.

"I'm fine," Iola insisted as Joe helped her up. She

looked at Callie and laughed. "You're the one who should see a doctor. You're as pale as a ghost."

"I thought I killed you," Callie said.

Frank started laughing uncontrollably.

"It's not funny!" Callie insisted.

"I know," Frank said, trying to stifle his giggles. "But look at Iola's hair."

Sure enough, the shock had made the hair on the top of Iola's head stand straight up.

"You look sort of like a fuzzy caterpillar," Joe said, and made a rough stab at smoothing Iola's hair.

Iola nodded at Callie, who gave Joe a playful whack in the chest. "Be nice!" she said.

The trainer arrived and helped Callie lead Iola to the training room for treatment. By then Montreux had fended off the news crew. She grabbed the arm of the fencer who was first to help Iola.

"Who set this stuff up, Victoria? It was you, wasn't it?" Montreux was so angry her voice trembled.

Victoria flushed. "You think I did this on purpose? You're crazy!"

The Hardys watched as Coach Sokal quickly stepped in. "All kinds of people have had their hands on this equipment in the past few days, Geneve. It was just a freak accident, I'm sure."

"But who's in charge?" Montreux asked. "Who's supposed to be in charge of fencing equipment?"

Sokal frowned. "Victoria," he admitted.

"And *you* hired her back," Montreux said. "So find out what happened and take care of it—now!"

Montreux strode off and Sokal followed her, pleading Victoria's case.

When they were out of earshot, Victoria muttered, "That's right. Always blame me." She picked up her mask and turned to look for her own weapon.

"Thanks for helping Iola," Joe said.

"No problem. I'm sorry she got hurt."

"So, you work for Coach Sokal?" Frank asked, curious about who might have had access to the fencing equipment.

"Yeah." The young woman tucked her mask under her arm and shook hands with Frank and Joe. She was small and compact, like a gymnast. Her blond hair was parted in the middle and hung down a few inches below her shoulders. "I'm Victoria Huntington," she said. "I used to be the number-one foil fencer on the Olympic team, but not anymore."

"Foil fencer?" Joe asked.

Victoria picked up her foil and showed it to Joe. "There are three fencing weapons," she explained. "The saber has a heavy blade with a sharp edge. The foil has a thin rectangular blade, no edge—"

"And the épée is even thinner, with a rounded guard to protect your hand," Frank added.

Victoria nodded. "Exactly."

"So why aren't you number one anymore?" Frank asked.

Victoria hesitated. "Well, let's just say Madame Montreux and I don't get along," she said finally.

"But you're here," Joe said.

"Barely," Victoria replied. "After Montreux forced me off her precious fencing team, Coach Sokal hired me to be one of his assistant coaches."

Frank took the foil from Joe and hefted it. "What does Montreux think of that?"

"She hates it," Victoria said. "Sokal leads all the junior teams—judo, fencing, archery, biathlon. But he mostly knows judo and archery. He needed someone who knew fencing to help him out."

Joe took a step toward the scorer's table and its bright red lights. "I want to check that stuff out," he said. "See how Iola got zapped."

Victoria quickly stepped in front of him. "Don't worry about it, Joe," she said.

"She is my girlfriend," Joe said sternly. "I tend to worry."

"This is my responsibility. I'll find out what happened."

"Maybe we can help," Frank said. "I know a little about electronics."

Victoria grabbed his sleeve. "I said, no thanks."

17

Seeing what was happening, Coach Sokal stepped over and calmly made Victoria release Frank's shirt sleeve. "What's the problem?"

"No problem," Victoria said. "I was promising Frank and Joe that I'd find out what happened with the scoring apparatus."

"Scoring apparatus?" Joe muttered. "More like a giant toaster."

Victoria glared at him.

"We just want to see the gear," Frank said, trying to keep Joe and Victoria from getting into a fight.

"Tell you what," Sokal said, "I don't think we want a bunch of people touching the equipment, possibly messing it up, right? So I'll take care of it myself." Sokal handed Victoria his clipboard. "Joe, why don't you see how your girlfriend's doing. And, Frank . . . hold on." Sokal waved another athlete over and introduced him.

"This is William Moubray," Sokal said, gesturing to a guy about Frank's age. He wore loose-fitting jeans, a white long-sleeved T-shirt, and a dark gray fleece vest with a U.S. Archery patch on the chest. "Moubray is one of the best archers on the junior team. He'll be happy to show you around."

"Absolutely," Moubray said.

"Just don't call him Bill," Sokal added. "He hates that."

Moubray smiled. "That's right."

Frank wanted to hang out with Moubray, but he couldn't help feeling as though Sokal was smoothing him over so he'd leave the scoring gear alone.

Joe trotted toward the training room, and Frank followed Moubray. When he glanced back, Sokal appeared to be ordering Huntington and another facility employee to pack up the equipment.

Moubray led Frank down a flight of steps to the basement of the training facility. "So how do you like this place?" he asked.

"It's great," Frank said, "but we've had a little too much excitement so far."

"Yeah, that incident was freaky," William said. "I've never heard of anyone getting shocked like that before. Come on, I'll show you our deluxe archery center." Moubray emphasized the word *deluxe* to make it sound as if he were kidding.

He was.

The basement of the training facility remained unfinished. Stacks of drywall, five-gallon paint drums, and piles of sawdust lined the walls. The space was still mostly open. A few offices and storage rooms had been framed in, but much of the floor was open space punctuated by round white columns.

William directed Frank around a corner to their right. There Frank saw what looked like an extra-wide hallway. It was so long Frank couldn't see all the way to the end. The long space faded into complete darkness.

William flipped a couple of light switches and illuminated the long space.

"This is our indoor target range," Moubray said.

Frank saw three archery targets down at the end of the wide hall, about sixty yards away. One of them had fallen over. Square signs marking the various distances to the targets hung from the ceiling.

"Is there really room for three people to shoot down here?" Frank asked.

William laughed. "No way, man. It isn't finished yet. Two people are the most you'll ever have down here at once."

"Unless you want to shoot each other," Frank said.

William nodded. "Montreux doesn't care too much about us archers." He pushed open a door at the head of the hallway.

"What do you mean?" Frank asked as they entered a small room lined with lockers and furnished with a couple of bare wood benches.

"She was a champion fencer," Moubray explained. "So she tends to give most of the money and attention to the fencers."

"That stinks."

"Yeah, I don't know if it's intentional or not. The

20

tiny indoor range doesn't bother me too much. I almost always shoot outside anyway," Moubray said. "But a few people are upset about how things are going here." He spun the lock on one of the lockers and withdrew two cases.

"Like who?"

"Oh, it's nothing serious," William said, placing the cases on a bench and zipping them open. "I figure this place is a whole lot better than nothing, so I keep quiet."

William withdrew the pieces of two complicated and expensive-looking target bows. Frank helped him screw the limbs to the lightweight magnesium grips. After that, a long stabilizer bar with counterweights was clamped on below the arrow rest. Finally, William calibrated and mounted the sights and, holding one limb between his legs, flexed the other one down, and strung first one bow and then the other.

"There," he said, handing one to Frank.

"Cool," Frank said. The entire bow weighed only a couple of pounds.

William then unlocked an equipment cage at the back of the room and got Frank a belt quiver to put around his waist, a bunch of target arrows, and a leather wrist guard.

"All right," William said. "Let's slide on outside."

"Outside?" Frank asked. "It's dark."

"Not a problem." William led the way up the stairs and out a back door. They stepped out on the opposite side of the building from the parking lot. The moon was only a sliver, and Frank couldn't see farther than ten or fifteen feet.

They walked along a recently paved path that curved into the woods behind the facility. About fifty feet in, they came to a clearing. William went to a stout aluminum pole and pulled a lever. Six sets of stadium lights snapped on, throwing an eerie yellow-green light over the outdoor range.

"Amazing," Frank said.

"This is more like it, huh?" William said.

Eight-foot corrugated steel walls enclosed an area the size of a football field. To keep stray arrows from hurting anyone, the range was carefully oriented toward a steep hill. The bright lights aimed down at them made the surrounding darkness darker, and the trees rose up behind the walls in long, spidery shadows.

William and Frank walked down to the fifty-meter marker. Frank could see his breath in the chilly fall air as he set his bow in a wooden rack and pulled on his wrist guard.

William went first. He took a pair of wraparound glasses from a vest pocket and put them on. Then he nocked an arrow, raised the bow, and pulled the arrow back in one smooth motion. His hand stopped right beside his nose and held there.

He became totally still. Finally, at the exact moment that Frank began to wonder when he would release the arrow, it was gone. It simply seemed to disappear from William's bow.

Frank heard a soft *thunk* and looked down the range to see William's arrow buried in the yellow bull's-eye.

"Sweet!" Frank said.

William adjusted his sight, then sent five more arrows into the heart of the target.

Frank tried to take his time. As soon as he had his arrow drawn, he noticed his heart beating. *Whump, whump, whump,* it went, making the tip of the arrow bob up and down. Frank held his breath and released. The arrow took off with a mild *thwang*.

It landed in the black area at the lower edge of the bull's-eye.

"Not bad," William said. He showed Frank how to make his release a little smoother by not using his thumb.

"And try to shoot between heartbeats," William advised.

"Yeah, right!" Frank said.

William laughed. "It takes practice, but you'll figure it out."

By his sixth arrow, Frank was into the blue circle, only a few inches from the center.

"You're on fire!" William said.

"I'll get the arrows," Frank offered. He set his bow in the rack and jogged down the range to the target. At one point he looked back at William, but the glare of the lights whited out everything behind him.

At the thick cork target, he pulled the arrows out one at a time. Most came out smoothly.

Frank pulled the last one out and turned to walk back. He thought he felt a bit of his hair lift at the side of his head, a breath of wind.

But the sound was unmistakable. He swiveled to look back at the target. An extremely thin arrow shaft protruded from the target, still quivering from the impact.

It had missed him by an inch.

3 A Pointed Message

Frank ducked low. He looked back toward William but was still blinded by the glare. Something buzzed past his ear.

Another arrow!

It sank into the gut of the target, so close Frank could have reached up and grabbed it.

He dove for the ground. "William!" he shouted. "William!"

He got no answer.

Frank lay as flat he could. He could smell the earth and the cold, frost-covered grass.

He thought to crawl behind one of the targets to

use it as a shield. But as he started crawling, the lights suddenly shut down.

The night went completely black.

Frank remained perfectly still. He heard a groan—a person falling, maybe—then the distinct sound of footsteps, of someone running away.

Frank scuttled back to the spot where he and William had been shooting arrows. He was ready to drop flat to the ground again. As his eyes adjusted to the darkness, he spotted William's bow lying in the grass. A few target arrows lay strewn around it. The arrangement looked like a dangerous game of pick-up sticks.

Frank fell flat again. He heard someone running, coming closer.

William burst out of the darkness, his chest heaving for air.

"Frank! Are you okay, man?"

"Yeah, but someone tried to ventilate me with a couple of target arrows."

"Me, too." William pointed to a spot on the ground a few yards away. The bright yellow shaft of an arrow stuck up out of the ground.

William picked up his bow as Frank pulled the arrow from the ground. "That was insane!" William said. "You dropped, then I see this shadowy outline of a person standing over there by the trail."

"I shouted your name," Frank said.

"I heard," William said. "At that moment I was diving for my life. Whoever that idiot was started lobbing arrows at me."

"Did you see who it was?"

William shook his head. He and Frank each had an arrow ready, in case their attacker returned. "I scrambled to turn off the lights," William said. "I figured we'd be safe in the dark."

"Good thinking," Frank said.

"Then I went after him, but I couldn't catch up."

Frank and William walked back to the target. Once they were close enough to see through the darkness, Frank noticed something he hadn't seen before.

"Check it out," he said. "One of the arrows has a note attached."

William withdrew the arrow and slid the folded square of paper over the tip. Holding it close, he read aloud: " 'Can't you take a joke? I could have hit you if I wanted!—Milli Le Walt.' "

"Who's Milli Le Walt?" Frank asked.

"No clue. Maybe the name is part of the joke."

"Some joke," Frank said.

"Yeah, I'm not laughing," William agreed.

The two teens turned on the lights again but didn't find any new clues.

William shut off the lights, and then he and Frank

followed the path back to the sports facility. Inside, visitors' night was still going strong.

Allen Frierson was showing a young girl how she could take down her older brother with a sweeping hip throw. The fencing strip where Iola had been injured was shut down, but the sound of swords ringing came from the other two. A burly coach held the end of a thick rope while a kid climbed the thirty-five feet to the top and rang a bell hanging from the rafters. His parents clapped and cheered.

Frank and William found the director of the center having a conversation with Bayport's mayor.

With a relaxed smile, Montreux introduced William to the mayor as a top hope for an Olympic medal in a few years.

"I already know Frank Hardy," the mayor said after he'd shaken hands with William. "He and Joe have helped me out many times."

Frank felt his face redden. He waited for the mayor to excuse himself to go talk to someone else before telling Montreux about the arrow attack.

"You're joking, right?" Montreux said, her face going slack with disbelief.

"I wish," William replied.

"Tell me everything you remember, but in my office." Montreux glanced around, apparently scanning the room for the news reporter.

The three of them left the gym floor, exiting through a set of glass doors. Old photographs from previous Olympic Games lined the hallway they entered.

Montreux's office was at the end of the hall. Inside, she motioned for the boys to sit.

"Whoever it was could have killed both of us," Frank said, flopping into a fancy armchair that seemed out of place in a sports complex.

"This is terrible," Montreux said. She toyed nervously with her lapel pin—a tiny gold foil. "First a girl almost gets electrocuted. Now this. The place is cursed."

Frank and William took turns telling Montreux all the details, including the note that claimed it was only a joke.

Montreux looked at William. "You know all the archers better than I do," she said. "Who might try something this stupid?"

"Nobody I can think of," William said. "I mean, even if it was some kind of sick joke, I don't think anyone would be that irresponsible. The first thing you learn as a competitive archer is safety measures."

There was a loud knock on the door. Without waiting for an answer, Coach Sokal stormed in. The veins in his thick neck bulged with exertion.

"Did something happen?" he asked. "I heard there was an accident on the archery range."

"How did you hear that?" Montreux asked.

"One of the guests saw a guy running into the building with a bow," Sokal said. "She said he seemed scared or hurt or something."

"What did he look like?" Frank asked.

Sokal had his hands on his hips. "I don't know. Scared or hurt or something—that's the only description I got."

Montreux raised her hands. "Calm down, Reid. I don't think anyone got hurt."

"But someone could have," William said. "There's a nutcase out there who thinks he's Robin Hood or something."

"Huh?" Sokal asked.

After Montreux filled Sokal in, he immediately wanted to call the police. "Geneve, I told you we were going to need security for this facility," he shouted. "If I was director, I would've hired a couple of cops for a busy night like tonight."

"*If* you were director, I'm sure you would," Montreux said bitterly. "I'm in charge, and I want this to be an open and fun place where people feel welcome."

"The flying arrows were a great welcome," Frank said.

Montreux glared at him. "Should I call the police?"

30

William looked at Frank. Frank shook his head. "No. It was probably a stupid joke," he said. Then more quietly, "Besides, I'd like to catch that coward myself."

"I'm with you there," William said.

Sokal's eyebrows shot up. "What?"

"Nothing," Frank said.

Montreux seemed relieved that Frank and William didn't want the police involved. "I want to talk to all the archers individually," she said to Sokal, "starting early tomorrow morning. We'll find out who did this, but I'd like to keep it quiet if we can."

"No problem," Frank said.

Back out on the gym floor, Frank thanked William and helped him break down both bows. Then he waded through the crowd until he found Joe, Callie, and Iola.

They were watching a demonstration of the scoring in biathlon, the combination of cross-country skiing and target shooting. A tall, blond young man was explaining how the round steel target switched from black to white when hit.

Frank asked Iola how she was feeling.

"I feel fine now," she said. "For a while my arm was tingling."

"I tried to get her to try fencing again," Callie said. "But she wasn't into it."

"How was archery?" Joe asked his brother.

Frank filled everyone in on his adventure.

"That's creepy," Iola said. "I think I'm ready to go home."

"When they say this is the Combat Sports Training Facility, they really mean it, don't they?" Joe said.

"Yeah," Frank agreed. "Tonight somebody took the name a little too seriously."

"I'm going over to thank Allen for the judo lessons," Joe said. "I'll meet you guys at the van."

Frank and the girls headed for the parking lot while Joe returned to the judo mats. Allen was close to the edge of one of the mats, doing sit-ups while his father held his feet.

"Sixty-five, sixty-six, sixty-seven . . ." Mr. Frierson was saying. "Come on, Allen. Suck it up."

Joe waited politely a few feet away. After the hundredth sit-up, Allen collapsed to the floor. His judo jacket was soaked through with sweat.

"Thanks for the lesson," Joe said.

"Hey, man. It was fun," Allen said, between deep breaths. "Come back anytime."

Mr. Frierson waved Joe away. "Some other time, kid. Allen's got a lot of work to do."

"Dad! Give him a break."

"Breaks don't make Olympic champions," Mr. Frierson said, his teeth clenched. "Coach Sokal won't put a slacker like you on his team. A hundred more sit-ups, now!" He placed his hands on Allen's feet again. "Let's go, get started!"

As Joe left, he saw Allen's nemesis, Jake Targan, coming out of the men's locker room. He was freshly showered and looked ready for an evening's entertainment.

Outside, Joe hopped in the van. It felt good to have a moment of quiet.

"Man, Allen's dad is tough," he said.

"Maybe that's what Allen needs," Callie said. "Someone to push him."

"Maybe," Joe replied.

The Hardys dropped Iola and Callie off at their houses. When Joe walked Iola to her door, he promised to call her in the morning to see how her arm was doing.

"And I'm going to find out if what happened was an accident or not," he promised.

"I'm sure it was," Iola said as she went inside.

Joe wasn't so sure, and he said so to Frank when he got back in the van.

"I don't know," Frank said. "Victoria was in no hurry to let us look at that wiring."

"Exactly," Joe said. "Then someone tries to make a bull's-eye out of your head. Something's wrong with that place."

Frank glanced in the rearview mirror for the third or fourth time in the past few moments.

"What's up?" Joe asked.

"I'm not sure," Frank said. "The same car's been right behind us for a long time."

Frank took a series of quick right turns, leaving and then circling back to their normal route home.

"Still there?" Joe asked.

"Nope. I'm just paranoid, I guess."

The Hardys came to their street, and Frank started slowing for their driveway. Up ahead, a set of headlights winked on, piercing the darkness. The lights came closer.

Frank had his turn signal on. It winked orange, off, orange, off.

The headlights moved closer, then angled toward the van. White light filled the windshield.

"What's that car doing?" Joe asked.

Frank slammed on the brakes. "Hold on!" he shouted. "It's coming straight for us!"

4 Who's the Hero?

Frank threw the van into reverse, ready to hit the accelerator and blast backward. With screeching tires, the other car jerked to a stop mere inches from the Hardys' bumper, blocking their driveway.

"Who is this fool?" Frank asked, holding his arm up to shield his eyes from the headlights.

"Let's find out," Joe said. He reached behind his seat and grabbed the best weapon he could find: an ice hockey stick. He and Frank leaped from the van, ready to defend themselves.

There was no need.

As soon as Joe was out of the van, he recognized the vehicle that had cut them off. It was also a van, white, with big red letters on the side: WBAY: Bay-port's Best News, First.

Joe tossed the hockey stick onto the passenger seat and squeezed through the space between the vans. He found Frank already being interrogated by Rachel Baden, the television reporter who'd been at the training center earlier.

She was wearing a powder blue jogging suit, perhaps to convince all the folks in TV land that she'd participated in the sports activities of the evening. But her curly red hair was no longer in a ponytail. It cascaded around her shoulders and would have been a serious problem in a judo match.

"What do you want, Rachel?" Joe asked.

"The truth," Rachel said with a wide smile. "That's all."

"Sure," Joe replied. "Something small you can blow up into something huge."

The cameraman stepped out of the sliding side door of the news van and hoisted the camera to his shoulder.

Rachel held up a hand, stopping him. "No," she said, tossing her microphone back into the van and pulling a miniature tape recorder from her jacket pocket. "No big production. Just a few questions."

"About what?" Joe asked.

"She thinks something happened at the sports complex tonight," Frank said.

Joe made his expression completely blank, as if to say, "What's she talking about?"

Rachel clicked on the recorder. "Frank, was there an incident on the archery range tonight?"

Frank glanced at Joe. They had promised Geneve Montreux they'd keep things quiet.

"I've got nothing to say," Frank finally replied.

"My source says you were almost killed, Frank. You've got nothing to say about that?" Baden persisted.

Frank shrugged. "Do I look dead? Am I hurt, even?"

"Someone didn't shoot arrows at you?" Rachel asked.

Joe stepped closer. "Who's your source?"

"Someone who sounds reliable, believe me." Rachel tucked a strand of hair behind her ear. "We packed up the van and left after the thing with Iola Morton," she said. "Then at the station we got a phone call. Anonymous. This guy had an interesting story to tell about you, Frank, and an archer named William Moubray."

"What, exactly?"

Now it was Rachel's turn to shrug. "If nothing really happened, then why do you care?"

"I don't like rumors," Frank said firmly.

"So tell me what you know. My source says poor design of the archery range may have been a factor."

"I don't think so," Frank said.

"So something did happen?"

"I didn't say that." Frank wanted to find out how much Rachel knew, so he tried to say just enough to keep the questions coming.

"Did Geneve Montreux try to save money on equipment? Are there other *accidents* waiting to happen at the Combat Training Facility?"

"We don't know what caused the fencing accident that injured Iola," Frank said.

"How much training have the coaches had?" Rachel asked. "My source claims the athletes are unsupervised. Is this true?"

"I don't know," Frank replied.

"One more question. Why were you and Moubray shooting at night? Isn't that dangerous?"

"There are lights."

"My source says the lights failed. That they went out while you were shooting and that's how you almost got skewered. Moubray, too."

"All I can say is that's not what happened," Frank said. "Did your source tell you anything about arrows?"

"No. Whose arrows? Tell me," Rachel said, holding the recorder out.

"Did your source mention a name?" Frank wanted

to know if Rachel's source had fed her the name on the note—Milli Le Walt.

"What name? Come on, Frank. What name?"

"I'm done," Frank said.

Rachel bit her lip in frustration, then turned to Joe. He just shook his head.

"Fine," Rachel said, stuffing the recorder in her pocket. She climbed into the news van. "Drive to Iola Morton's house," she said to the cameraman. "We'll get a shot of her bandaged shoulder. Then cut to Montreux saying it was only a little accident. The audience will love it."

The van backed up, then roared down the street.

Inside the house, Frank and Joe found their mother, Laura Hardy, sitting in the living room, reading a gardening magazine. She had the television on, which, apparently, had kept her from hearing any of the commotion outside.

She looked up and smiled. "Hey! How was the new training place, or Olympic Center of Combat . . . whatever it's called?"

Joe laughed. "Combat Sports Training Facility, Mom."

"It was great," Frank said. He didn't want to worry his mother by telling her he'd spent the evening dodging arrows. "Joe got pummeled by a black belt in judo. That was especially fun."

"Oh, honey. You didn't get hurt, did you?"

"No way," Joe replied, though his wrist was still kind of sore. "Just hungry."

"There's stuff for sandwiches in the fridge," Mrs. Hardy said.

As Joe started toward the kitchen, he pulled Frank aside for a second.

"I'm going to call Iola and warn her that Rachel's on her way over," he whispered.

"Good idea," Frank said. He then flopped down on the couch next to his mom. "Where's Dad?"

"He got a call this morning from a company out in California," Mrs. Hardy said. "Someone's been hacking into their computers."

The Hardys' father, Fenton, was a well-known private detective. He often took off to work on a new case on a moment's notice.

"He'll be back early next week," Mrs. Hardy said.

"Cool," Frank said. He pointed to the television. "Turn the sound up when the news comes on, Mom," he said. "We might be on there."

"Oh?"

"Yeah. They were at the training facility for the big event tonight."

"I'll be sure to watch," Mrs. Hardy said.

Claiming he was tired, Frank headed upstairs to his room.

About ten minutes later Frank heard *and* smelled his brother coming up the stairs. Joe tromped in with a plate loaded down with a hot turkey and pepperoni sandwich, chips, and a heavy slice of chocolate cake.

"You act like you haven't eaten all day," Frank said.

"I'm a growing boy," Joe replied. He sat at Frank's desk, while Frank lounged on the bed.

"So," Frank said. "Where did Rachel Baden get her information?"

"Well," Joe said around a mouthful of turkey and pepperoni. "She said the anonymous caller was *some guy.* I guess that means it was a man."

"That doesn't fit with the name Milli Le Walt on the note," Frank said. "At first I thought it might be the practical joker trying to get some publicity."

"Except that the caller didn't mention the note to Rachel," Joe said.

"Right." Frank stared at the ceiling. "The tipster basically pointed the finger at Geneve Montreux—"

"Accusing her of mismanaging the training center," Joe added. "Of running a dangerous facility."

"And it might be true," Frank said. "That thing with Iola was pretty bad."

Joe crunched a mouthful of chips. "I still want a look at those wires. I don't care what that Victoria person says."

"I agree," Frank said. He sat up and ticked off the

fingers on his right hand as he named names. "Who knew about the incident with William and me? Me, William . . . then we told Montreux. And Coach Sokal said a woman saw someone run into the building with a bow."

"What about William Moubray?" Joe asked. "Do you really believe his story?"

"What story? You mean when he said he didn't realize what was going on until someone took a shot at him?"

"Yeah," Joe said. "What if he's Milli Le Walt? He could've taken a couple of shots at you, then drilled an arrow into the ground to make it look like someone was after him, too."

Frank finished Joe's thought. "Then he runs over and turns out the lights so he can be the hero."

Joe dug into his cake. "You said he complained that Montreux gives everything to the fencers and cheaps the archers. This works out perfectly for him. He pretends to save you, then calls in an anonymous tip to make Montreux look bad and make himself the hero."

Frank held a hand up to his chin and thought for a second. "That would make perfect sense if the snitch had told Rachel exactly what William told me—that he saved me by turning out the lights. But Rachel said her source told her that the lights were faulty. That they went out by themselves."

"I guess you're right," Joe agreed.

"And Rachel didn't say anything about William being a hero," Frank added. "Only that he almost got hurt, too."

"If his only motive was to make Montreux look bad, then what?"

Frank frowned. "Then it's possible he did do it. Took some dangerous shots at me, then called the press to put his own spin on it."

The next morning Laura Hardy stood in the kitchen with her hands on her hips, looking exasperated. "Frank," she said, "I watched the news last night as you asked me to."

"Oh, yeah?" Frank said. "Did you see us?"

"Yes, I did. And I saw poor Iola lying on the floor like a dead person."

"She's fine," Joe said, pouring milk into a bowl of cereal. "I called her this morning."

"Good," Mrs. Hardy said. "They said something else on the news, too."

Frank raised his eyebrows, waiting.

"They said there was some kind of accident on the archery range but that they'd been unable to confirm anything."

"You know they always exaggerate that type of thing on the news, Mom," Joe said.

"Well, if you boys are going back over there, be careful," Mrs. Hardy said, shaking a finger at them.

"Of course, Mom," Frank said. "Don't worry."

Laura Hardy said she would try not to, but other parents didn't seem to be able to. By the time the Hardys arrived at the training facility, a group of seven or eight reporters and twenty or thirty parents had cornered Geneve Montreux on the front steps.

As the Hardys approached the giant, clam-shaped building, they could hear people shouting questions.

"Ms. Montreux! Did you rush to open the complex too early?" a reporter yelled.

"No. I don't think so," Montreux said.

"Is it true someone's going around shooting arrows at people?"

Montreux backed up toward the glass doors. "No. No, that's not true at all."

A parent's question got cut off when Allen Frierson burst out of the front doors, almost knocking over Montreux.

"Th-there's . . . inside!" he stammered. "Ms. Montreux, there's an emergency inside!"

Montreux stared at him in shock and horror. "What?"

"Some kid. He's stuck . . . he's going to fall any second!"

Someone gasped.

The reporters and several parents rushed to the doors, trying to shove their way in.

As the doors swung open, desperate cries rose from inside.

5 Rafter Rescue

Once inside, the Hardys both knew there were only a few moments to spare. A boy, thirteen or fourteen years old, was desperately hanging from a rafter.

"He must be twenty-five feet off the floor," Joe said.

"Thirty," Frank corrected.

An area of the huge main gym behind the judo mats had been designated the Upper Body Conditioning Center. It included a steep climbing wall, a wooden peg board, and the climbing rope to the steel beam rafters.

The rope had obviously broken. It lay on the floor under the boy in a tangled coil.

"He's barely hanging on!" a man shouted.

A woman pointed to the ceiling with one hand, while she covered her mouth in horror with the other. She turned when they all came rushing in.

"Someone call Nine-one-one!" she screamed. "The fire department! We need the fire department!"

"There's no time!" Joe said.

The boy kicked his legs wildly, trying to maintain his grip on the hard metal.

"Hurry!" he shouted. "I'm slipping!"

Beckoning for everyone to help, Frank began dragging the judo mats over to place them on the floor under the boy.

Joe sprinted out to the van. He wrestled the sliding door open. Tossing things aside—hockey stick, walkie-talkie headset, motorcycle helmet—he finally found what he needed.

Joe slung the rope of his grappling hook over his shoulder and hefted the three-pronged grapnel. "This is that kid's only chance," he muttered to himself.

In the distance Joe could hear sirens. The fire department was still minutes away as he rushed back inside.

"Hurry, Joe!" Frank shouted. The stack of judo mats was about a foot high, enough to break the boy's fall, but not enough to prevent serious injury.

Frank waved everyone back to give Joe room.

Holding the slack rope loosely in his left hand, Joe began spinning the grapnel in his right.

"No way this will work," someone said.

The kid tried to hoist himself up, but he was way too tired. "Hurry!" he cried.

Joe had to get the rope close enough so the kid could grab it, but . . . Joe's stomach suddenly did a tumble as he imagined himself hitting the boy with the heavy steel hook and bringing him down. That would be a terrible disaster.

Everyone around him seemed to take a deep breath.

Joe released the hook. It hummed through the air. Perfect . . . be perfect, Joe thought.

The hook clanged off the rafter and dove to the floor like a wounded bird.

"No!" someone gasped.

Quickly Joe yanked the grapnel back. He didn't have time to worry about neatly coiling the rope. He took a step back and spun the hook again, concentrating on the empty space above the rafter. He let go.

The rope sang through his hand as the grapnel arced toward the ceiling.

A cheer went up as it sailed over the rafter and bounced loudly off the floor.

"Okay!" Joe shouted to the kid, anchoring the rope. "Grab the rope and climb down!"

The kid tried to slide along the rafter to the rope. "I . . . I can't," he stammered. "I can't make it."

Without hesitating, Joe handed the rope to his brother and started climbing. At the top, he glanced down for a second. At least twenty faces were staring up at him in silence.

Holding on with one hand, Joe reached over and pulled the kid toward him. The boy shook with fear. With Joe's help, though, he was able to make it to the rope and hang on.

Slowly, resting every few feet, the two of them made it safely down. As their feet hit the ground, firefighters came bursting in the front doors.

The boy's mother ran up and hugged him. Frank slapped Joe on the back. "That was amazing, man!"

Geneve Montreux fought through the crowd. "Thank you, Joe," she said. "Your quick thinking probably saved that boy's life."

"It was nothing," Joe said modestly.

With everyone gathering around to shake Joe's hand and thank him, Frank quietly walked over to the climbing rope to take a look at it.

He knelt down and stared at the lower end of the rope. Carefully, he checked it for fraying. Everything was fine until he got to the metal cap and hardware that secured the rope to the rafter.

This is where it broke, he said to himself. Scanning the floor, he found the locking hook, similar to a mountain climber's D-ring, that had been at the top of the rope. It had failed, breaking open and bending so much that it had slipped from the eyebolt in the rafter.

Frank rubbed his thumb over the cracked end. He couldn't be sure, but it might have been tampered with.

Someone snatched the D-ring from his hands. Frank looked up. Rachel Baden stood over him, holding the hardware aloft.

"I found it!" she said loud enough for everyone to hear. "This is why that kid almost died. More faulty equipment."

Frank stood up and grabbed the D-ring back. "Quiet!" he said. "We don't know why this happened yet."

It was too late. Parents and other reporters swarmed around the coiled rope like ants attacking sugar. Rachel had her mini-recorder out and was holding it under Geneve Montreux's nose. "This place has been open for only two days," she said, her voice hard with accusation. "And there have been at least two accidents, maybe three. What's going on?"

"We need time to figure this out," Montreux said weakly. To Frank she appeared tired. Worry lines creased her forehead, and her voice was hoarse.

In all the commotion, Frank pocketed the metal part and pulled his brother from the crowd.

"I say we take this opportunity to have a look around," he whispered.

Joe nodded. They slipped through the gym doors leading to the long, office-lined hallway.

"So, what did our friend Rachel find?" Joe asked.

Frank made a wry, half smile. "She didn't find anything." He pulled the D-ring from his pocket. "*I* found this."

Joe took the part and examined it. "Could those be file marks?" he asked.

"That's what I was wondering. We'll need to take a closer look later."

They passed a series of poster-size black-and-white photographs from previous Olympics. One was an action shot showing Coach Sokal standing behind an opponent who was kneeling on a mat. Sokal had his left arm hooked under the other guy's left armpit and snaked around the back of his neck.

51

He had his right arm clamped across his opponent's throat.

"Take a look," Joe said. "That's a brutal single-wing choke hold."

"Not something you escape from," Frank said. "Come on. Let's check these offices."

Sokal's office was on the left side of the hall, just before Montreux's, which was at the end of the hall.

"Here," Joe said, pointing to the nameplate on the office one door before Sokal's.

Victoria Huntington, it said.

Frank glanced back down the hall. It was empty.

"Locked," he said.

"I've got sweat pants on," Joe whispered. "I don't have my lock picks."

Frank stepped to the next door, Sokal's office. "Locked."

"Not this one," Joe said. He stood smiling by Montreux's open door. "With all that's happened this morning, she must've forgotten to lock it."

The Hardys silently sneaked inside and closed the door. Frank headed for the antique desk, while Joe rifled through some files in an expensive-looking cherry filing cabinet.

"I've got something!" Frank said, standing up from the desk. He was opening a file of papers.

Joe stepped over and peered over his brother's

shoulder. The first page was titled "Letter of Official Dismissal."

Frank read parts of the letter in a low voice.

"Dear Victoria,

"Though you are an extraordinarily gifted fencer, I feel you have left me no other choice than to dismiss you permanently from the U.S. Olympic Fencing Team.

"You claim that the recent injuries suffered by other athletes were accidents. I disagree and hold you personally responsible."

"And blah, blah, blah," Frank said. "It's signed by Geneve Montreux."

"Wow!" Joe exclaimed. "Sounds like Victoria's a troublemaker."

"Sure does," Frank agreed. "I wonder what kind of injuries she caused."

The file also included Victoria's appeal to the United States Olympic Committee. But they had sided emphatically with Montreux, calling Victoria's actions "dangerous."

"Appeal denied," Joe said.

Frank placed the file back in the desk.

"So we know Victoria and Montreux pretty much hate each other," Joe said. "What now?"

"We check out Victoria's office," Frank said matter-of-factly.

"You want me to go back through that crowd to get my lock picks?" Joe whispered. "That'll take forever. And besides, Montreux, Sokal, or anybody could come down the hall and catch us red-handed."

"Don't freak." Frank pointed at the ceiling. "Why go through a door when you can drop in from above?"

Joe looked up and saw a brand-new drop ceiling. All they had to do was push aside one of the tiles, climb up through the hole and over the wall to Sokal's office.

"Good call," Joe said. He rolled Montreux's office chair close to the wall Montreux shared with Coach Sokal.

While Frank climbed up on the chair, Joe peeked out the door to make certain no one was coming.

"We're still clear," he whispered.

A loud noise made Joe turn around. He expected to see that Frank had taken a tumble off the chair.

Frank was fine, though. He was still standing on the chair, his arms poised over his head. There was a dark gaping hole in the ceiling where he'd moved a tile aside.

The objects that had caused all the noise lay on the floor beside the chair legs.

"The fencing equipment from Iola's accident?" Joe said.

"Yeah," Frank agreed. "But what is it doing hidden in the ceiling?"

6 Foiled

Frank jumped off the chair. With his toe he pushed away the cardboard box the equipment had been in and knelt down.

"What exactly do we have here?" Joe asked, kneeling next to his brother.

Frank pushed his brown hair away from his eyes. "Evidence."

"What's this thing that looks like a giant electric train transformer?" Joe asked, poking at a white plastic box with a couple of switches and a voltmeter on top.

"The junction box. Be careful how you touch it," Frank added. "We're going to have to try to put all this back exactly the way we found it."

"Junction box?"

Frank nodded. He pointed to the two fencing vests that lay crumpled on the floor and the long, very thin black wires that would connect them to the white box. "The retractable wires are attached to circuits in the box," he explained.

"But I didn't see any box when Iola got shocked."

"It sits under the scorer's table," Frank said. He gently untangled two more, shorter, wires. "These wires go from the box to the red lights on top of the table."

"But how do the lights go off?"

"You know how one of those big flashlights works, right?" Frank asked. "You've got a battery with a positive end and a negative end. A wire runs from each end to the lightbulb."

"Oh, yeah," Joe said. "If you pull one of the wires off its end of the battery, the light goes out."

"Right. The circuit is broken."

"This works the same way?"

Frank nodded. "Each fencer has his or her own lightbulb, right? Your vest is hooked into the positive end of your circuit, and my foil is connected to the negative end."

"When I touch your vest with my weapon, your light goes off because I completed your circuit."

"You got it," Frank said.

While Joe checked the door again, Frank rummaged around in Montreux's desk until he found a dime he could use to open the transformer box.

"Here we go," he said, lifting the bottom panel off.

"What do you see?"

"Nothing," Frank said.

"You mean . . ."

"Somebody ripped the guts out of this thing," Frank said.

Joe pointed at Frank. "As if they were getting rid of incriminating evidence."

Frank began replacing the fencing stuff back in the cardboard box. "Montreux is trying to cover up Iola's accident," he said.

"If it was an accident."

"If it was an accident, then she's trying to cover it up to protect her position as director of the training facility," Frank said. "And if it wasn't an accident, then something even more serious is going on."

"We've got to find the missing electrical parts," Joe said. He steadied the chair while Frank placed the box back in the ceiling and moved the tile back in place.

The brothers moved the chair below a different tile and scaled the wall to Sokal's office from there.

"Wow! This is different," Joe said as he dropped lightly on to the hard tile floor of Sokal's office.

"I'll say. *Warm* and *friendly* aren't terms that come to mind."

The coach's office was completely different from Montreux's. Instead of a thick woven carpet and antique furniture, Sokal had a cold gray ceramic tile floor and gray steel office furniture. His office was also a huge mess.

Joe pointed to a section of judo mat leaning up against the wall.

"What's he got that for, I wonder," Frank said.

Joe went over and tipped the mat down to the floor. "Sokal must use it to school his athletes," Joe said with a laugh. "You know. There's no time to walk all the way out to the gym to show somebody a new move, and words don't make the point as clearly as you want." Joe did a one-arm shoulder throw on an imaginary opponent. "That's what you should've done during the match yesterday, you lazy idiot!" Joe imitated Sokal perfectly.

Frank laughed, then both brothers became silent when they heard a noise from the hall outside.

Joe put an ear to the door and a hand on the doorknob.

"Somebody out there?" Frank asked.

Joe shook his head. "I don't think so." He tilted the mat against the wall again.

The Hardys began their search. Frank went through a pile of rumpled judo uniforms in the corner. There was nothing hidden underneath them.

Joe found a stack of archery targets folded up in one desk drawer.

"Bull's-eye," Joe joked. He held up a target. It had six holes right through the yellow center.

"Good shooting," Frank said. "Hey, is that somebody's name written on the edge there?"

Joe peered at the border of the target. "Yeah, it is. Your friend William Moubray must've shot this bad boy full of holes."

Frank and Joe went through the rest of the targets. Each one had an archer's name and a date on it, recording how well he or she had shot that day.

"No Milli Le Walt, of course," Frank said.

"Nope, but look at this." Joe pointed to a set of five targets with the initials *R. S.* scrawled across the bottom.

"Reid Sokal?" Frank asked.

"Without a doubt," Joe said. "He's aces with a bow and arrow, man. Only a couple of shots in all these goes outside the bull."

"He coaches all the junior teams," Frank said. "I'd expect him to know a little about archery."

"Agent Reid Sokal," Joe mocked. "A black belt in judo, expert archer, fencing master extraordinaire."

"Not quite," Frank said. "Remember, he hired Victoria to coach the junior fencers because he's no good at it."

"Oh, yeah," Joe said. He put the targets away and went to the metal filing cabinets. Sokal had a file on every athlete he coached.

Joe thumbed through a few of them. "Hey, Frank," he said. "Listen to what Sokal has to say about Allen Frierson."

"What?"

" 'Athlete is highly motivated and tough,' " Joe read, " 'but lacks talent. His background in wrestling has helped him gain strength, but he does not have the balance to be successful in judo at a high level. Cut from team before new facility opens this fall.' "

"Harsh," Frank said.

"Yeah, but something happened," Joe said. "It's dated six months ago. Obviously he didn't cut Allen before the training center opened."

"Maybe he saw more improvement than he expected," Frank noted.

Joe replaced the file. "That's cool. Good for Allen."

Frank walked around the room, pushing up on each ceiling tile. "I don't see anything, Joe," he said. "We should check out Victoria's office. We're running out of time."

Joe agreed. He pointed at a framed print on the wall behind Sokal's desk. "That is the only nice thing in here," he said.

Frank glanced at it as he climbed into the ceiling

to head for Victoria's office. The painting showed a man in medieval clothes with a longbow drawing a bead on a young boy. The boy stood next to a tree and had an apple on his head. Neither of the two seemed to be happy about the situation.

"The legend of William Tell," Frank noted.

The two brothers dropped easily into Victoria Huntington's office.

"That's the guy who decided to show off by shooting an apple off his son's head, right?" Joe asked.

"He wasn't showing off," Frank said, scanning Victoria's office. "He was a hero in Switzerland seven hundred years ago. Switzerland was at war with Austria. And the Austrian king, Albert I, had this steward named Gessler."

"Steward?"

"The dude who's in charge of the king's official affairs," Frank said.

"Oh," Joe said, trying to open a closet next to Victoria's filing cabinets.

"But get this," Frank said. "Gessler ordered everyone to salute his hat. Not him, just his lousy hat."

"No way!"

"Yup. When Tell refused, Gessler made Tell's son put an apple on his head and then he told Tell to shoot it off."

"What a nightmare."

"What a shot," Frank said.

"Bingo!" Joe said after he opened the closet door!

"What did you find?" Frank asked.

"A fencing outfit, a couple of sabers, a foil, an épée, and, behind these shoes, some very complicated electronics," Joe replied.

Together, he and Frank pulled out the tangle of wires and circuit boards.

Frank spread everything out on the desk. "Iola's accident was no accident," he said.

"Victoria rigged it?"

"I'll say," Frank answered. "The wires from the foils and vests are supposed to go through these circuits that draw very little current."

"What did she change?"

"She bypassed the boards all together. Iola was basically plugged straight into the wall outlet of the gym."

"So when Callie touched her, she got zapped."

"Big time," Frank said.

Joe let out a whistle. "I'd say Victoria has it in for Montreux. She did this to make the director look bad and then hid the stuff in the ceiling of Montreux's office. If anyone found it, they'd think Montreux was trying to cover something up."

"Makes sense to me," Frank said. "We have our saboteur."

Joe watched as Frank's eyes went wide with alarm. "What?" he whispered.

"I think I heard a key in the door," Frank said.

Joe spun toward the office door. The knob was turning slowly. "Hide!"

There was nowhere to go. Frank tried the closet, but it was full of stuff.

Joe pulled the office chair out, prepared to dive under the desk.

The door swung open. Victoria's jaw dropped in surprise. "What are you doing in here?" she cried.

Frank held his hands up in attempt to calm her. Joe stepped away from the desk.

In a flash Victoria's expression switched from surprise to rage. She darted to the closet, reached in, and pulled out a foil.

The blade whipped through the air as Victoria turned to face the Hardys. "I said, What do you think you're doing?"

"We caught you," Joe said.

"Quiet, Joe," Frank said.

Victoria didn't seem to understand.

Frank didn't want to make her any madder. "We can explain this," he said. He tried not to let his eyes focus on the mess of wires on the desk but couldn't help himself.

Victoria saw what he was looking at, and her expression changed again.

"Are you trying to set me up? Is that it?" she screamed.

Joe took a step toward Victoria as she rushed at him, her foil extended. Before either brother could react, the tip of the foil pierced Joe's side.

Victoria jumped back.

Joe still had his hands up. He stared down at the side of his sweatshirt where a spot of blood bloomed.

7 Emergency Alarm

Victoria dropped the foil, which clattered to the floor.

"You stabbed me." Joe's eyes were wide with disbelief.

"I . . . I didn't mean to," Victoria said, her voice quavering. "You walked into my foil." She sank to her knees.

Frank kicked the foil across the room and settled at Joe's side. He lifted his brother's sweatshirt gently. "You've got about a three-inch cut under your ribs," Frank said.

"Oh, no. Oh, no," Victoria said. "This couldn't have happened. The point is blunt on a foil." She leaned forward to get a look but winced and sat back down on the carpet.

"It happened," Frank snapped. He focused on Joe. "The cut isn't deep at all, he said to Joe. Frank had a T-shirt on under his fleece pullover, and he took that off, using it as a compress to stop the bleeding.

"Hey! What did I miss?"

Frank glanced up to see Rachel Baden at the door.

"Oh, my gosh!" she said. "Joe's hurt!" She rushed into the room.

"What are you doing here?" Joe moaned.

"I followed Victoria from the gym," Rachel said. "Oh, man. If only I'd gotten here a minute earlier, I would've seen everything!"

"Try not to be too disappointed," Joe said sarcastically. He sat up gingerly and, with Frank's help, settled into a wooden chair.

"Make yourself useful," Frank said. "Call an ambulance."

"And the police, right?" Rachel asked as she picked up the phone on the desk.

Frank stared at Victoria. She seemed truly upset by what she'd done to Joe. But he was a witness. She'd stabbed him on purpose. "Yeah, call the police, too," he said.

Victoria suddenly stood up and went for the foil.

Figuring she planned to attack and make an escape, Frank leaped to his feet. He started for her, hoping he could disarm her with a karate kick before she could do any more damage.

Victoria picked up the sword, and as she was about to wheel and face him, Frank settled into his stance. His muscles tensed. He prepared to deliver an arm-breaking side kick.

Victoria turned and held up a hand palm out, asking Frank to stay cool.

"Look," she said, deliberately handing the foil to Frank. "The end is sharp. Someone filed it to a point."

Flank studied the end of the sword. Sure enough, the metal safety button had been filed off. It was now sharp and deadly.

"You didn't do this?" Frank asked.

"No! Absolutely not," Victoria said. "This wasn't my fault. I wanted to give you guys a scare, sure, for breaking into my office. But all my weapons have buttons. I had no idea I could actually hurt your brother."

Rachel had finished her call to the police and hung up the phone. She got to Victoria's closet before Frank could.

"That's a nice story and all," Rachel said. "I doubt it's true, though." She pulled the weapons from the closet one by one and handed them to Frank. "All these are as sharp as razors."

"Yikes! I guess I was lucky," Joe said. "If she'd slashed me with a saber, my guts would be all over the floor."

"But I didn't do that," Victoria protested. "Don't you see, somebody else must've broken in here and filed the blades. They wanted to make me injure someone."

Two paramedics and a police officer came running into the office, followed by Geneve Montreux and Coach Sokal.

"What's this?" Sokal asked, noticing the electronics on Victoria's desk.

"That's proof," Joe said as the paramedics dressed his wound.

Frank explained the story to the police officer, starting with how the sabotaged fencing equipment had shocked Iola and ending with Victoria's stabbing Joe with the sharpened foil.

"That's not true!" Victoria shouted. "None of it's true."

"You'll get a chance to tell your side," the officer said. "At the station."

Sokal paced the room, looking at Victoria with scorn. "You betrayed me," he said. "I brought you back after Geneve dismissed you. Now this is what you do?"

"That's not all," Joe said. He then explained about

the rest of the fencing rig hidden in the ceiling of Montreux's office.

Sokal volunteered to retrieve the stuff. When he returned and dumped it on Victoria's desk, Frank explained his theory.

"We think she was about to set up Geneve Montreux," Frank said. "Make it seem like she was trying to cover up evidence about the accident."

"This is insane!" Victoria shouted.

"No," Montreux said bitterly. "You, young lady, are the one who seems to have lost it."

The paramedics were ready to take Joe to the hospital, so everyone cleared out of the room. The officer strung crime-scene tape across the door until more officers could come to pick up the evidence. Sokal and Montreux, trailed by Rachel Baden, headed to Montreux's office. "Do you think either of you could have prevented this?" Frank heard her asking.

Frank followed Joe and the paramedics down the hall for a moment. He tapped his brother on the shoulder. "I'll meet you at the hospital," he said.

After lingering in the hall until it was empty and quiet, Frank quietly padded back to Victoria's office.

If she filed her weapons to sharp points, then where is the file? he wondered.

Ducking under the yellow tape, he entered her office and shut the door most of the way behind him.

He went through each desk drawer. Nothing. On the floor of the closet he zeroed in on the several pairs of shoes he had seen before.

When he picked up a white tennis shoe, something tumbled out to the floor.

A diamond-hardened file.

Frank picked it up. Pulling the D-ring from his pocket, he compared the ridges on the file to the marks on the metal. "A perfect match," he muttered. "That means Victoria damaged the D-ring, too."

Twenty minutes later Frank tracked Joe down in the hospital. Mrs. Hardy was already in his room, watching as a doctor stitched up his side.

"Frank, I thought I told you two to be careful," Mrs. Hardy complained.

"I was careful," Frank said. "It was Joe who decided to challenge someone armed with a three-foot sword."

Mrs. Hardy held her face in her hands. "Oh, I can't believe it," she said. "Wait until your father hears about this one."

"Just tell him we closed another case," Joe said. "That's all he needs to know."

"So all those accidents at the training center were caused by one person?" Mrs. Hardy asked.

"We think so," Frank said.

"This young woman, Victoria Huntington," Joe

added. "She had it in for the director, Geneve Montreux."

"That's terrible."

"Well, it's over," Joe said. "We can all relax."

Frank wasn't so sure, but he kept his thoughts to himself.

"All done," the doctor said, standing up.

"How many stitches?" Joe asked.

The doctor laughed. "That's what everyone wants to know. Nine on the inside and a few more than that on the outside."

"Excellent!" Joe said.

Mrs. Hardy cringed. "I don't think it's something to be so happy about."

"He'll be fine, Mrs. Hardy," the doctor said. "He's had a tetanus shot, and we also want to put him on IV antibiotics tonight to prevent infection. He can go home tomorrow."

Joe fiddled with the electric bed controls, tilting himself up higher. "Thanks, doc."

The doctor left, and a nurse and an orderly came in. While the nurse set up the rolling IV hanger, the orderly unpacked Joe's lunch.

A gray piece of something that looked sort of the right shape to be meatloaf swam in some grease next to yellowish carrots and a watery cup of chocolate pudding.

"Smells like burned rubber," Joe said, holding his stomach.

"Don't look at me," the orderly said. "I just deliver the stuff."

Mrs. Hardy picked up her purse. "I'll go get something for you," she said. "How about a large pizza?"

"Mom, that would be perfect," Joe said. "And get one for Frank, too."

Laura Hardy laughed. "I'll be back in a little while."

After the nurse and orderly left, Frank set a chair next to Joe's bed and clicked on the television.

He found the twelve o'clock news. "Check it out, Joe," he said. "We're the top story."

"Cool."

The brothers watched as the news anchor went through the events of the past two days. Behind her, on a superimposed screen, the station showed shots of Iola's injury, followed by footage of Victoria Huntington being led into the Bayport police station by two officers.

"I'm getting word right now that a press conference has been called at the Olympic Combat Sports Training Facility," the anchor said. "Let's go there live."

The picture switched to a full-screen shot of Geneve Montreux standing behind a podium in the training center's crowded press room.

"I've called you all here today to explain the things that have gone on over the past two days," Montreux said. She continued on, in a tired voice, to review the events.

"I'd like to thank Frank and Joe Hardy personally," she continued. "They were instrumental in helping us find out who was behind the incidents here."

Joe held his hands up and high-fived Frank. "Sweet!"

"And finally," Montreux said. "The United States Olympic Committee met a few minutes ago and asked that I resign my position as director of the Combat Sports Training Facility."

"Pretty severe," Frank said.

Montreux paused and tugged at the cuff of her jacket. "I want to emphasize that I did not intentionally cover up any of the incidents here. But in the interest of helping the training center get off to a new start, I have agreed to resign. Coach Sokal, the coach of the junior teams, will take over as director immediately."

As Montreux stepped back from the podium, Sokal came forward, a big grin on his face.

"I don't have that much to add right now," he said. "I plan to make a few initial changes to get this behind us and make the training center a safe, fun place to visit. I hope we'll see you all here soon."

Frank switched off the TV and leaned back in his chair, letting it hit the wall next to Joe's bed.

A series of loud beeps shot out of Joe's electronic monitor.

"What in the . . ." Frank jumped up from his chair.

Green and red lights flashed on and off next to Joe like an overloaded supercomputer.

Two nurses sprinted in.

Joe looked up at his brother. "Frank, am I dying?"

8 William
Telltale Clues

A nurse pushed Frank to the side roughly. "Let me get next to him," she said.

Joe had his hand on his heart. "I think I'm okay," he said. "Really."

The second nurse pushed a button on the vital signs monitor. The lights and noise stopped.

"Of course you're all right, sweetie," she said.

The first nurse had her hands on her hips. "Your brother here leaned on the emergency call button," she said.

"Sorry," Frank said.

The nurse put one hand on Frank's shoulder and turned him toward the wall behind Joe's bed. With the other hand she pointed to a blue button surrounded by a red light. "See that button?" she said.

Frank nodded.

"Stay far away from it."

Joe and the second nurse laughed as Frank took his scolding.

As the two nurses left, Callie and Iola came in.

"Hey, how'd you know I was here?" Joe asked.

"Your mom called from a pizza place," Iola said, sitting down in a chair on the opposite side of the bed from Frank and Callie. "She said I should come tickle you in your side." Iola threatened Joe, holding her hands up and wiggling her fingers.

"No, stay away," Joe said. "Ouch!" He held his side. "And don't make me laugh either."

"Oh, all right," Iola said. "I'll be totally serious."

"Impossible," Callie said.

"Like Victoria being innocent," Frank added.

Iola's eyes shifted from Frank to Joe. "You mean . . ."

"It wasn't an accident," Joe said. "Victoria Huntington fixed it so you would get a nice shock when Callie scored a touch."

"Why me?" Iola asked.

"I don't think she picked you," Frank said. "Whoever put on that fencing vest was going to get fried."

"She wanted to embarrass Montreux," Joe said.

Frank pulled the D-ring and metal file from his pocket. "And I found this file in Victoria's office after everyone left," he said, filling the girls in on the rope incident.

"And look at this," Joe said, taking the D-ring from Frank. "See how the metal has turned bluish close to the clamp?"

Frank nodded.

"Metal does that when you heat it with a blow-torch or something."

"You think Victoria tried to weaken the metal by heating it?" Callie asked.

"She must not have been sure the file thing would work," Joe said.

"There's only one thing that bothers me," Frank said. "Who fired those arrows at me."

Callie's eyes went wide. "Someone shot at you? Why didn't you tell me?"

"I'm telling you now," Frank said. "It was last night, about half an hour after Iola got shocked."

"Well, it wasn't Victoria Huntington," Iola said.

"How do you know?" Joe asked.

"You should know, too, bonehead," Iola said. "You guys were all with me in the training room."

"Hey, that's right!" Callie said. "About fifteen minutes after Iola's accident, Victoria came in to see how she was doing."

"She said she'd just finished packing up the faulty equipment and promised to check it out as soon as she could."

"The girls are right, Frank," Joe said. "Victoria was still in the training room when we left, asking the trainer to look at her sore knee or something."

Frank put the file and D-ring back in his pockets. "Case not closed," he said. "Victoria must have had an accomplice."

"Someone who's still out there," Joe said.

Late that afternoon Frank pulled the van into a parking lot close to the Combat Sports Training Facility.

Joe still suspected that William Moubray had deliberately shot arrows at Frank, then set himself up to be the hero. Frank was here to pay him a visit.

Moubray lived in a dormitory for athletes who had traveled long distances to train at the center. It was a flat-roofed, two-story brick building that resembled a prison as much as a dorm.

The white winter sun was going down as Frank went in. He found a row of mailboxes inside, with William Moubray's name listed under Number 206.

He took the steps to the second floor two at a

time. He came to a landing, opened a heavy fire door, and entered a long, carpeted hallway so narrow he could hold out his arms and almost touch both walls.

A couple of athletes stood outside their rooms, talking. Rock music blared from someone's stereo, and Frank could smell chicken soup cooking.

The door to Room 206 was open, throwing a square of light into the hallway. Frank found William inside, stirring soup over an electric hotplate.

"Frank," William said. "What's going on, man?"

"Not much," Frank replied.

"That's not what I hear," William said, spooning up a taste of hot soup. "Word is Victoria put your brother in the hospital. Is he going to be okay?"

"He'll be fine," Frank said. "I just came by to get your take on all this stuff."

"You know more than I do," William said. "Victoria stabbing your brother—was that what finally got Montreux canned?"

Frank nodded as he sat down on Moubray's bed. He noticed how bare the room was. The cinder-block walls were painted a dull, off-white color, and William had only a couple of posters up. One showed a jazz trumpeter playing on a darkened stage, the other a lone cross-country skier cutting a trail through some woods.

"Did you know Victoria at all?" Frank asked.

"Want some soup?" William asked.

"No, but thanks," Frank answered.

William turned his desk chair around and sat. "I knew Victoria pretty well," he said. "That's why I'm so surprised about all this."

"What do you mean?"

"I mean she's tough and has an attitude and all, but I never figured she'd try to mess with Montreux like this."

"It was pretty crazy," Frank said.

"Oh, yeah," William agreed. "She's lucky nobody got seriously injured."

Frank leaned forward on the edge of the bed. "What did happen between Victoria and Montreux?"

"I don't know the whole story," William said, taking a sip of soup. "From what Victoria told me, Montreux made junk up to get her kicked off the team."

Frank remembered the letter he and Joe had found in Montreux's office. "I thought Victoria injured some people or caused some kind of accident."

"Victoria's totally intense," William said, "just like the rest of us. She goes all out in practice every day."

"What's so bad about that?"

"Nothing," William said. "But one day Victoria is practicing with this other girl, and Vicky is dominating so bad it isn't even funny. She attacks and runs the girl off the back of the fencing strip. The girl blows out her knee and is gone for a year."

"Sounds like bad luck to me," Frank said.

William shrugged. "The other girl was one of Montreux's favorites. When Montreux tried to give Victoria coaching advice, Vicky would sometimes ignore it. You know, she likes to find her own way."

"So Montreux kicked her off the team?"

William placed his soup bowl on his desk. "That's the way I heard it. Montreux got tired of dealing with Victoria and exaggerated some stuff so she could justify kicking her off the team."

"No wonder Victoria was mad," Frank said.

"Yeah, I'd be mad, too," William said.

For the first time Frank noticed an old, beat-up gun case in the corner of the room. It was wide enough to hold ten or twelve rifles, and the glass panels that had been in the door were missing. Frank stood up and went over to it.

"You mind?" he asked.

"Go ahead," William said. "All my important stuff goes in there."

Though he could see inside already, Frank swung the door open. A brutal-looking crossbow hung against the back wall. "Oh, man," Frank said. "This thing is serious."

William stood up. "Take her out," he offered.

Frank lifted the weapon and held it to his shoulder, aiming at the skier in the poster.

William held up a short arrow with a steel head that looked like a giant shark's tooth.

"Brutal," Frank said as he took the crossbow bolt from William and turned it, looking at every angle. "That could take out just about anything."

"I almost never shoot it," William said. "It's too easy . . . and too dangerous."

"I bet," Frank said, returning the bow and bolt to their places. As he did, he noticed a bundle of target arrows at the bottom of the case. They appeared to be exactly like the ones that had been shot at him. Frank said nothing.

"Here," William said, pulling an oil cloth off a target air rifle also in the case. "You set a dime on its edge, I can hit it with this thing from a hundred yards."

"Impressive," Frank said. "I see you've got cross-country skis, too."

William nodded. "I'm getting into biathlon. Just for kicks."

"Where you ski like a hundred miles with the rifle on your back and then shoot out a bunch of targets?"

William laughed. "Yeah, but it's a lot more fun than you make it sound, and Coach Sokal encourages it. I'm staying in great shape."

"I guess you're glad Sokal's going to take over for Montreux," Frank said.

William glanced at Frank suspiciously. "Yeah, I suppose."

Frank closed the door of the case. "He seems like a good guy."

"Oh, Sokal can be a jerk, just like anybody else," William said. "But at least the archers will get some attention now. You know, even though Sokal's a judo champion, he's also a great archer. I've seen that dude practically split one arrow with another, like Robin Hood."

Frank recalled the targets Joe had found in Sokal's office. "Yeah, that's pretty cool."

Frank kept thinking about the arrows and the fact that William didn't like Montreux. He didn't seem like a person who would pull the kind of dangerous stunts that had forced Montreux to resign, but he certainly had a motive to get rid of her. He could definitely be the person who helped Victoria. Frank decided to keep a close eye on him.

"I don't know anything about biathlon," Frank said. "I can hold my own on cross-country skis, though."

"You want to hit the trails? They're making snow," William said happily. "That would be great."

"How about tomorrow?" Frank said. "I'll meet you here."

William held out his hand, and Frank slapped his against it. "Excellent!" William said. "I'll ski you into the ground, Frank."

"Bring it on, Moubray." Frank was about to leave when the sight of the target arrows popped back in his head. He pivoted and went to William's desk.

"What is it?" William asked.

"Hold on," Frank said. He'd remembered the print of William Tell in Sokal's office. Taking out a scrap of paper and a pencil, Frank wrote down the names *William Tell* and *Milli Le Walt*.

He began crossing out all the letters in the two names that matched. In seconds he was left with nothing. *Milli Le Walt* was an anagram of *William Tell*.

"What are you up to?" Moubray asked.

Frank crumpled the paper. "What do you know about the legend of William Tell?" Frank asked.

"Not much. Ask Coach Sokal, though. He talks about it all the time."

"Oh, yeah?"

"Sure. It's his favorite motivating tool," Moubray said. "Whenever archers have a crucial match, Sokal

85

tells them to imagine that the life of the person they love the most is on the line with each shot."

Three, maybe four, loud popping noises interrupted them.

"What's that?" William asked.

"It came from the hall."

Frank and William ran from the room. Shouts came from a room down the hall, followed by a billowing cloud of black smoke.

9 An Unsanctioned Match

Glancing down the hall, Frank saw Jake Targan stumbling from one of the rooms, his arms clasped over his head for protection. Leaning over, he went into a spasm of violent coughing.

"Fire!" he gasped.

Staying low, Frank and William braved Targan's room.

"It's the curtains!" Frank shouted. Orange and yellow flames climbed the curtains, snapping and crackling as they rose.

With one forearm covering his eyes, William yanked the curtains to the floor. Frank whipped the comforter from Targan's bed. He tossed it over the burning heap, then jumped on top, stomping the fire out before it could rage again.

Puffs of smoke curled from under the comforter. Soon the fire was completely extinguished.

The stink of burning cloth filled the room.

"Nice work, guys," someone said as Frank and William stepped back out into the hall.

"Yeah. William, you could always join the fire department if archery doesn't work out."

"No thanks," William said, rubbing his hands together.

"Get burned?" Frank asked.

William blew on his fingers. "It isn't bad. I'm fine, man."

Targan brushed past them. He returned from the room carrying his charred hotplate by its half-melted cord. He held it at arm's length like road-kill.

"The thing practically exploded," he said.

Allen Frierson pushed through the crowd of athletes. He wore a jacket and ski cap. "What are you cooking, Jake? Whatever it is, it stinks."

"Very funny, Frierson," Targan said.

"Who's trying to be funny. I hope you're going to clean this up so everyone else doesn't have to deal with this smell all night."

"Take it easy, Allen," Frank warned.

"What're you worried about?" Targan said to Frierson. "Go stay with your daddy. You don't have to smell anything."

"Shut up about my dad!" Frierson shouted.

"You shut me up!" Targan retorted.

Before Frank could step between them, Allen was at Jake's throat like a wild dog.

When Allen lunged at Jake, Jake ducked, slamming his shoulder into Frierson's gut. Allen let out a loud grunt.

Everyone but Frank backed off to give the two athletes room to fight. He reached in, getting a good grip on Targan's shirt. "Break it up!" he yelled. "Break it up!"

Frank felt a couple of pairs of strong hands wrap around his arms and pull him back.

"Let go!" he said. "What're you doing?"

"Give them room," Moubray said, his hand on Frank's shoulder.

"Let them settle this," the judo heavyweight on the other side of Frank said.

The athletes had formed a tight circle around Frierson and Targan. No one said anything. The only sounds were of the fighters hitting the floor and the sirens from the fire house in the distance.

Frierson was on his back swinging away with

roundhouse punches. Targan ducked his head as punches rained on his skull and ears. Reaching in, he grabbed Allen in a bearhug. Then, with heavy punches still landing, he took his forehead and struck it against Frierson's.

Frierson screamed as Targan ground bone against bone. Frierson stopped punching to use his hands to shove Targan off.

Targan scrambled around so he was kneeling at Frierson's head. Like a rodeo cowboy wrapping the legs of a thrown calf, Targan snatched Frierson's right arm and secured it under his right armpit. His left arm coiled around the back of Allen's neck, locking him in a reverse strangle hold.

"Get off me!" Frierson screamed.

"Submit," Targan said calmly.

"Get . . . off . . ." Allen's voice broke in a dry cough as Targan squeezed.

"I don't want to hurt you," Targan said. "Give in and I'll let go."

They all held a collective breath.

Finally Frierson slapped the ground with his free hand, the signal that he was giving in.

Jake immediately released him and stood up.

His face red with embarrassment, Allen clambered to his feet. He grabbed his ski cap and ran from the dorm.

"What was that all about?" Frank asked.

"Nothing," Targan said with a sigh.

"I thought you two were friends," Frank said.

The heavyweight fighter still at Frank's side said, "You should mind your own business, man."

Frank took a step forward, but Moubray cut in. "Relax, everybody. Frank's cool. And this isn't the kind of welcome we want to be giving visitors to the dorm."

"I'm going out to eat," someone said. "Who wants to go?"

A chorus of me's went up. The crowd dispersed as athletes returned to their rooms for coats and wallets.

Targan stepped into his room. Frank picked up the damaged hotplate and followed.

"Sorry about that," Targan said. He tried to smooth the wrinkles in his shirt, but a button had been torn free.

"So, can you tell me what the problem is?" Frank asked.

"Allen's under too much pressure," Targan said. "Did you know his dad quit his job so he could be here in Bayport with Allen? He rides Allen all the time. Work harder, be tougher."

"Did something happen today? Something to set Allen off?"

Targan nodded. "I don't know the details, but I think Coach Sokal told Allen that he doesn't have talent and that he might be cut from the team."

Frank remembered the file in Sokal's office, the one with notes about cutting Frierson before the combat center opened.

"I guess he took the news hard," Frank said.

"Wouldn't you?" Targan asked. "He's completely upset. He's picked fights with me all day. I just let it go, figuring he needed to let off steam. Unfortunately, I let him get to me this time."

Frank set the hotplate on the scorched desk. Most of the evidence was melted, but Frank could clearly see where plastic insulation had been stripped from a couple of wires, leaving them exposed.

"What are you looking for?" Targan asked.

"I don't really know," Frank replied. "Make sure the fire department takes a look at this."

"Sure," Targan said. "And thanks for helping put out the fire."

"No problem." Frank left as a firefighter came down the hall.

"We got a call that the fire was already out," he said. "Mind if we take a look?"

Frank jerked a thumb back toward Targan's room. "In there," he said.

* * *

Night had fallen when Frank returned to the parking lot. Light from the fire truck parked in the fire lane behind the building flashed on the trees, making them pulse red for a second then go dark.

He found the van and unlocked the door. As he was about to get in, he felt someone grab his shoulder. He wheeled around, ready to fight.

It was Victoria Huntington, looking tired and cold in jeans and a fleece pullover. She had her hair tucked under a baseball cap.

"Victoria," Frank said warily.

"Don't worry," she said, holding her hands out. "No sharpened swords, see?"

"I see," Frank said. "I was about to head home."

"I need to talk," Victoria said. "I mean, I just spent like six hours talking to the police, but now I need to talk to you."

Frank closed the van door. "The cops said you were free to go?"

"I'm not under arrest," Victoria said. "I can't leave town, though. They're still investigating."

"Okay, so let's talk," Frank said.

Victoria nodded toward the dorm. "Can we take a walk? I need to move."

"That's cool," Frank said. "I wouldn't want anyone to hear us."

Victoria stuffed her hands in her pockets as they crossed the parking lot.

When they were a safe distance from the dorm and combat complex, Victoria broke the silence.

"I went by the hospital to visit Joe," she said. "He told me you might be here."

Frank didn't say anything.

"He says he's going to be fine," Victoria said. "Not even much of a scar."

"Yeah, that's good," Frank said.

Victoria finally blurted out, "I'm innocent. I told Joe first and now I'm telling you. I have no idea how that scoring equipment got in my office, and there's no way I sharpened my weapons."

Frank wanted to believe her. He knew she couldn't be the person who shot arrows at him, but evidence against her for the other incidents was so strong. He thought about the poster of William Tell in Sokal's office.

"What about Coach Sokal?" he said.

"What about him?"

"Could he be involved?"

Valerie shook her head. "I'm not going to say anything against Coach Sokal. He saved me after Montreux kicked me off the team."

"Why did he do that?" Frank asked.

"He knew what she was doing was unfair,"

Victoria said defiantly. "He knows how hard I worked to get here, and he needs someone to coach the junior fencing team. That's why he did it."

"Okay, okay," Frank said. "It just seems to me that he had a motive to try to get rid of Montreux, just like you."

"What motive?"

Frank steered them back toward the van. "He seems pretty happy to be the new facility director. Maybe he wanted Montreux's job all along."

"He was disappointed when she was named director, I know that," Victoria said. "But not as disappointed as some other people."

"Like who?"

Victoria sighed. "After what's happened to me, I don't want to say anything bad about anyone else."

"Name names," Frank said. "I've got a metal file that makes it look like you rigged the rope to break. That kid could've been killed."

Victoria stopped. "Frank, you've got to believe me. I would never do anything like that!"

"Who would?"

"William Moubray," Victoria whispered. "He hates Montreux."

"That's a strong word."

"She ignores the archers," Victoria said. "She

barely considers it a sport. Believe me, Moubray's a nice guy, but he does not like Montreux at all."

They were back at the van. "I'll look into it," Frank said.

"Thanks." Victoria disappeared into the darkness.

Frank got out his keys but realized he'd left the van door unlocked when he went on the walk with Victoria. He climbed in, thinking over all the details of the case.

He gunned the van's engine and pulled out of the parking lot. If Sokal wanted to be director of the training center, then it made sense that he and Victoria would set things up to make Montreux look bad. But if Victoria was innocent, as she claimed, who was Sokal's accomplice? Was it Moubray?

And what about Sokal? His mission had already been accomplished. He was the new facility director, so there was no longer any reason for him to sabotage Jake Targan's hotplate and cause a fire. That would only be counterproductive.

A light snow began to fall, the delicate flakes sticking to the windshield. Awesome, Frank thought. A good snow that night would add to the pack the snow machines had put down already. He and William might even be able to blaze their own trails through the woods.

Frank switched on the wipers and glanced in the rearview mirror. What he saw made his heart jump in terror.

A man in a black ski mask was crouching behind his seat, red-rimmed eyes coldly staring back at Frank in the mirror.

10 Hospital Horror

The man in the ski mask leaned forward, placing a gloved hand firmly around Frank's throat. "Listen to me, and listen good," he whispered hoarsely. "It's over. Victoria Huntington's the one. You caught her, now leave it alone!"

"Let go of me, punk!" Frank said. He threw his right arm back and connected with hard cheekbone.

"Ahhgg!" The man tightened his grip on Frank's throat.

A burning pain made Frank twist in his seat. The van swerved on the slick road, headlights catching the houses along the quiet street.

Frank pushed back at the guy with his right hand

while steering with his left. The van swerved back the other way, going up on three wheels, then jolted to a stop against the opposite curb.

Frank lurched against the steering wheel. The masked man tumbled forward between the front seats.

Recovering, Frank clawed at the door handle. The door popped open, and he rolled out onto the street.

His attacker followed, leaping nimbly from the van.

Joe sat up in his hospital bed eating a bowl of orange Jell-O. Callie and Iola had left before dinner. Mrs. Hardy had stayed most of the afternoon and evening but finally left, promising to return in the morning.

After finishing his food, Joe reclined the bed, clicked off the TV with the remote, and reached over to switch off the lights.

The room was nice and dark. A row of tiny LED lights scaled the IV dispenser like a glow-in-the-dark centipede. Dull red lights on the bedside monitor registered his pulse.

He tried sleeping on his side, but that was too painful. Rolling over on his back, he sank his head into the pillow and closed his eyes. It had been a long day.

He drifted off, thinking of nothing for a long, long time.

Then he had a dream. At least he thought it was a dream. He was swimming. The water was warm, but he needed to come up for air. The water was very deep, so deep no light broke through. He was in total darkness.

He needed air. Kicking his legs and pulling at the warm water with his hands, Joe struggled to make it through the dark to the surface and the light.

Then he knew he was awake. He was awake, but he couldn't breathe. His lungs burned. Something, a pillow, was being pressed down on his face.

Joe yanked at it with his hands. It didn't budge, and even more terrifying, he felt a pair of strong hands holding the pillow down.

He kicked wildly, tried to yell. No sound came out. Still the pillow smashed into him, crushing his nose, his eyes, filling his mouth.

He felt himself losing consciousness. In desperation, he reached behind the bed. Clawing at the wall, he found the emergency call button and pressed.

The weight disappeared. Joe ripped the pillow off his face.

A shadowy figure ran from the room, bowling over a nurse as she opened the door.

Joe lay back in the bed, gasping for breath. "No false alarm this time," he said to the nurse.

She stared at him, stunned.

* * *

Frank sprang up from the ground, expecting the guy in the mask to come right at him. His attacker hit the pavement lightly and paused as if trying to decide what to do.

Frank threw a spinning back kick. Coming around, he waited for the jolt of contact when his heel hit its mark. It didn't come. Out of the corner of his eye, he saw his opponent duck neatly under the blow.

Frank remembered to hold his hands high: the finish of a spinning kick always left you open for a straight right.

He needn't have worried. The man had taken off, sprinting up the street across front lawns so he'd be out of the streetlights.

Frank wasn't about to let this coward escape. If he didn't want to stay to fight, Frank would take the fight to him.

At top speed, he dashed after the guy.

They crossed three lawns, leaping hedges like high hurdlers. Closing in on a picket fence, Frank's prey jumped too early. Frank watched as the guy tried to extend his lead leg over the pointed boards. His toe caught, and he flopped headlong into the next yard, skidding on the snow-slicked grass.

Frank dove. Clearing the fence with ease, he landed right on top of the guy in the mask. With one burly arm, the guy threw Frank off.

Watch yourself, Frank thought as he rolled to his feet. You don't want to get too close and get into a wrestling match with someone this strong.

The two opponents faced each other on the snowy lawn. "Take off your mask, mystery man," Frank said. "Or are you so ugly I'd fall over dead when I see you?"

The guy just shook his head. He lunged at Frank, trying for the judo hold that could finish Frank in mere seconds.

Frank stood up straight, waiting. A split second before his attacker made contact, Frank lifted his right leg and swung it in a high, half-moon arc. The outside of his shoe cracked into the side of the man's face.

The guy crumpled at Frank's feet.

Blue and red lights illuminated the snow. Frank glanced over to see a police cruiser skid to a stop at the curb.

An amplified voice boomed, "Freeze, Bayport police!" Two officers jumped from the car.

Frank bent down to remove the man's ski mask. The two officers were on him, shouting, "I told you to freeze, kid!"

Frank went down, tackled by the cops. They rolled across the new snow. He didn't give the officers any resistance. "It's Frank Hardy!" he shouted.

Frank felt himself being lifted to his feet. He held up his hands, making it clear he wasn't a threat. He scanned the ground, but the guy in the mask was already up and gone.

"Frank?" It was the Hardys' friend on the Bayport police force, Con Riley.

"The guy on the ground attacked me," Frank said.

The other officer took off, following the tracks in the snow.

"Sorry, Frank," Riley said. "We got a call from one of these houses. They said some guy was getting chased. When we pulled up, I thought you were some criminal about to seriously hurt that guy."

"He hid in my van," Frank said, pointing up the street where the van sat, still idling against the curb.

The other officer returned, out of breath. "Lost him," he said. "Lost his prints in the woods back there."

"Oh, man," Riley said. "I guess we let him get away."

"I wanted to get his mask off," Frank said, "to see who he was."

Con and the other officer walked Frank to his van. "Try to stay out of trouble, Frank," Con said. "If you have another run-in with that character, give us a call. Meanwhile, we'll drive around the neighborhood in case he comes out of the woods."

"You know I always call when I'm in trouble," Frank said with a smile. "That is, when there's time."

"Which there never seems to be," Con said. "How convenient."

Frank waved goodbye and drove off. Instead of going home, he figured he should head to the hospital to check in with Joe. It was late, but he figured he could talk his way past the nurses for a visit.

To Frank's surprise, he had no trouble getting in to see his brother. In fact, the nurses seemed relieved to see him when he stepped off the elevator on Joe's floor.

The first thing he noticed was the police officer standing outside Joe's room. The guy was big, so big that he looked stuffed into the bullet-proof vest under his uniform shirt.

Then, as he got closer, Frank spotted his mother behind the cop. She was talking and moving her hands a lot, something Frank knew she did when she was upset, which was pretty rare.

When he approached, Frank heard the end of their conversation.

"Just don't feel that I can go home, now," Laura Hardy was saying.

"Believe me," the cop said. "Your son will be safe now. I'll be here until the shift change in the morning."

"Oh, Frank!" Mrs. Hardy said as Frank came up. "You're safe. I've been calling everywhere."

"I'm fine, Mom," Frank said, giving her a hug to reassure her. "Why the guard for Joe?"

"He had a visitor," the officer said. "An unwelcome visitor."

"It's awful," Laura Hardy said. "Joe seems okay though. He keeps telling me to go home."

Frank could tell his mom was working hard to keep her composure. She almost never lost it like this.

Frank went into the room. He found Joe watching the tube and sucking down a large milkshake.

"What flavor?" Frank asked.

Joe took one last slurp and then gave the barrel-size cup a satisfied look. "Chocolate, what else?"

"I should've guessed."

"Hey, did Mom tell you what happened?"

"No," Frank said. "But she looks pretty upset. What did you do?" he teased.

"What did *I* do?" Joe said. "I almost managed to get myself suffocated by an untamed killer pillow."

"No way!"

"Absolutely, man. I wake up with some fool trying to make me eat this thing," Joe said, holding up his pillow.

"Did you see who it was?" Frank asked.

Joe shook his head. "The lights were out, and I was just trying to get some air in my lungs."

He told Frank how the emergency call button had

saved him. "Whoever it was ran over the nurse like a fullback, but she didn't get a good look at him either."

Frank, careful to be sure his mother was still outside the room, related his story to Joe.

"At least now we can be sure it's two people," Joe said. "While I was munching pillow stuffing, you were fighting some guy all the way across town."

"And it means Victoria probably isn't involved," Frank said. "Unless . . ."

"Unless what?"

"Unless she asked me to go for a walk so the guy in the mask could sneak into the van and wait for me to get back."

"You mean we've got three criminals?"

Frank put his hand to his chin. "It's possible. The guy who attacked me was definitely a judo expert. Who do we know who fits that description?"

"Allen Frierson," Joe said. "And Coach Sokal and—"

"But I still don't get it," Frank said, interrupting. "Sokal is director now. If things go wrong at the center, he gets kicked out, just like Montreux."

"So it's not Sokal," Joe said. "It could be Frierson or anyone on the judo team."

Frank stared at the floor, thinking.

"We still don't trust Moubray," Joe said. "Are you sure he's not involved?"

"No, I'm not," Frank said. "Apparently he hates Montreux as much as anybody."

After telling Joe good night, Frank convinced their mom to go home. Joe would be safe with that great bear of a cop looking out for him.

The next morning was Sunday. Frank got up early and peered out his bedroom window.

"Excellent!" he said. At least four inches of fresh snow had fallen during the night—nice light powder, perfect for skiing.

He packed up his skis and drove to the athletes' dorm. Inside the building, he stomped the snow from his boots and clapped his gloved hands together to warm them.

The second floor was quiet. Only a slight smoky smell remained to remind Frank of what had happened the evening before.

He went to room 206 and knocked on the door. No answer. He peered under the door. No light. It was almost as if no one was around. He knocked again, louder.

Still, no answer.

A door opened down the hall. Frank turned. Jake Targan came out of his room, skis in his hand, and a target rifle slung over his shoulder.

Frank felt his hands go clammy with sweat. Targan

was certainly a judo expert. He could have attacked Frank the previous night.

Targan walked toward Frank, unslinging the rifle as he did.

Frank squared his shoulders to face Jake.

"Looking for William?" Targan asked.

"Yes," Frank said.

"He's not in, obviously," Targan said.

Frank expected Jake to level the rifle at him any second. Targan stopped a few feet away and swung the rifle around, offering the stock end to Frank.

"Here," he said. "Moubray's waiting for us at the trail. He asked me to give this to you."

Frank took the rifle. "What for?"

"He said you'd need it," Targan replied.

11 Cross-Country Combat

"I hope he meant I'll need it for target shooting," Frank said.

Targan smiled. He handed Frank a box of .22 caliber pellets and a cartridge of carbon dioxide for the air rifle. "The way things have been going, you never know."

"I'm not late, am I?" Frank asked. "Is that why Moubray took off already?"

"No. Right on time," Jake replied. "William seemed to be in a big hurry when I saw him this morning. He got some kind of phone call, but I don't know what was up. This is all he talked about last night, though, so I'm sure we'll catch up to him on the trail."

Frank checked the safety on the gun and swung it over his shoulder. "I didn't know you were into the biathlon, too," he said.

"I'm not," Jake replied. "I don't shoot, but I love to ski. You don't mind if I go along, do you?"

"Of course not."

Once outside, Jake pulled on a red candy-striped stocking cap. "It's cold, man. That's the only thing I don't like about skiing. You can't do it in the summer."

"This isn't cold," Frank said. "Wait until January. Now, that's cold."

Targan slid his skis into the back of the van, and Frank drove inland from the bay toward the only mountains close to Bayport. They weren't mountains, really. More like long, sloping hills. But with good snow, the miles of trails made for fun skiing. Downhillers had to pay for lift tickets at the lodge. Cross-country enthusiasts merely entered the park area and drove to the lot next to the trail head.

They entered on a narrow gravel road. The snow had made the city streets slick. Here, though, the tires grabbed well on the snow-covered rocks and dirt.

No one was in the little information hut at the park entrance so early on a Sunday morning, so Frank drove on through the raised wooden gate.

110

"There's William's car," Jake said, pointing to a silver hatchback.

"It's the only other car in the lot," Frank observed. "He shouldn't be too hard to find."

Frank maneuvered the van next to Moubray's car. He and Jake jumped out.

"William!" Frank shouted. "William!"

No one answered.

"Maybe he's warming up," Targan said. "As competitive as he is, I bet he wants to ski us both into the ground."

"Let him try," Frank said, grinning. He opened the back doors of the van and unloaded their skis. Within a few minutes they were both locked into the bindings of the long, narrow cross-country runners.

Frank hoisted the rifle over his shoulder. He then stabbed his poles into the ground and slid the skis back and forth. His bindings were working nicely.

"Ready?" Targan asked, pulling yellow-tinted goggles over his eyes.

In answer, Frank took off. He strode forward, his legs slightly bent at the knee. His arms and legs soon fell into a smooth rhythm. He glided over the snow, arms swinging like pendulums and legs pushing, then recovering.

They reached the wooden sign at the end of the parking lot. It read, Bay Ridge Trail, 12.5 Miles.

111

"Tracks," Frank said, noticing the two thin lines worn into the fresh snow. "William must've already started."

"Let's catch him," Targan said. "You up for it?"

"Just watch," Frank said. He charged ahead through the leafless trees.

Frank felt the cold air expand his lungs. The sun was out, and the snow glistened and twinkled in the light.

He ducked under a fallen tree branch. "Watch your head!" he called to Jake.

"Got it," Targan replied.

Frank took the trail as fast as he could. Up hills, he had to splay his skis like a duck and walk his way to the top. He could hear Jake behind him, the *shush* of the skis on the snow and the bite of each pole digging into the ground.

"Watch your speed on this hill," Frank called.

He tucked his poles behind him as he leaned his way between the too-close tree trunks. Then it was down a steep hill. Frank went into his tuck and picked up speed.

Fifteen, twenty, twenty-five miles an hour. Pine trees whistled past. The skis tracked and bounced over rocks beneath the snow. Coming to a curve, Frank leaned into it, brushing a thorn bush with his shoulder.

He heard a ripping sound behind him. "You okay?" he called.

"This is great!" Targan shouted. "Don't slow down. That bush got part of my jacket, that's all."

The ground leveled out. Frank slowed and pushed his way into a clearing. He skied up to a railing set on two posts just off the trail.

"The first target area," he said as Targan plowed to a stop next to him.

"You're good on the skis, Frank," Targan said. "What can you do with that gun?"

The wooden railing marked the spot to shoot from. A hundred meters away, a metal frame held six black disks barely as big around as a softball.

"Those targets look about as big as ants' eyeballs from here," Targan said.

"They're big enough," Frank replied. He pulled a plastic magazine holding five pellets from the butt of the rifle. He inserted it and lifted the rifle to his shoulder.

Taking a deep breath, he squinted through the scope. His eyes watered from the cold. The crosshairs blurred. He floated the sight just above the first black spot, then held his breath. He squeezed the trigger. A second later a metallic clank echoed back to them.

"Nailed it!" Targan said.

The first black spot in the row had flipped over to white.

Frank carefully pulled off five more shots. On the last one, a muscle in his shoulder twitched. No clank.

"Aw, that one went high," Frank muttered. "Missed the entire thing."

"Five out of six," Targan said. "That's still great."

Frank slung the rifle back over his shoulder. Grabbing his poles, he pulled toward the main trail.

"Hey, Jake," he said.

"What?"

"Where are William's tracks?"

They stopped. The snow on the trail was fresh and unblemished.

"I don't see them," Jake said.

"But we didn't pass him," Frank said. "So where did his tracks go?"

Targan shrugged. "He must have turned off somewhere."

"I guess," Frank said.

"Keep going," Jake suggested. "We'll find him soon."

Frank slid back onto the trail, cutting grooves in the snow. He figured Moubray must somehow still be ahead of them. Putting his head down against the wind, he picked up the pace.

He stared at the tips of his skis. They ate the snow like the prow of an arctic icebreaker. Frank watched as a neat round hole about the size of a quarter opened up in the snow in front of him.

What was that? he thought. A raindrop?

Then he heard a distant, muffled crack—a rifle shot. Another hole appeared in the snow, inches from the tip of his ski.

"Frank!" Targan called.

Frank slowed and glanced over his shoulder. Jake was pulling with one pole and pointing to the left with his other.

Frank looked in that direction. He saw what Jake saw, a man standing off on a far rise. He was leveling a high-powered rifle in their direction.

"I see him!" Frank called. "Follow me!" Frank cut between two thick trees. A bullet ricocheted off one, spitting bark and ringing past Frank's head.

"We're sitting ducks!" Targan shouted.

Frank charged ahead. He lungs felt as if they were about to explode. When they came to a fork in the trail, Frank chose the branch that headed downhill. They needed speed.

"We're okay," Targan said. "I can't see him anymore."

"Is it Moubray?" Frank shouted.

"I don't know, Frank," Targan replied. "I guess I don't know the guy as well as I thought."

They zipped downhill, wind tearing at them. At

the bottom of the slope, the trail made an unexpected turn to the left. It carried them around, then around some more. Soon they were headed back in the direction from which they'd just come.

"This is bad," Targan said.

Frank was about to stop and backtrack when the gunman jumped out from behind a tree right in front of them. He rammed his shoulder into Frank, sending him sprawling and his air rifle spinning through the air like a baton.

Frank watched as Targan coolly kept his speed. He chopped at the guy with his ski pole as he shot by.

The gunman doubled over in pain. Frank was about to cheer for Targan when Targan skied into an exposed root and flipped over, skis flying.

Frank kicked off his cross-country skis and stared down the gunman. The man was tall and wore a black ski mask and a long, duster-style brown overcoat. His boots were soaked through from the wet snow.

The gunman swung his arm around, shaking off the blow from Targan's ski pole. As he lifted the rifle to aim, Frank bolted toward him. If he could get close enough, the man wouldn't be able to get off a shot.

Frank couldn't get his legs to work fast enough. They felt heavy from skiing, and his boots slipped on the snow.

He got close to the gunman but not close enough. Right before he collided with the man, Frank felt something hard and heavy slam into his stomach. The wind shot out of him. With a moan, he doubled over and crashed to the frozen ground.

He looked up at the bright sky. Am I shot? he wondered. Pulling his hands away from his belly, he saw they had no blood on them. He realized he hadn't been shot; the guy had nailed him in the solar plexus with the butt of the rifle. He tried to speak, but there was no air in his lungs.

Frank watched helplessly as the gunman walked slowly over to where Jake lay, his right ski stuck under his body.

"You're done with judo for a while, superstar," the man growled. He then brought the rifle stock down hard on Jake's right arm.

Targan let out a yell.

Frank got to his knees, then fell forward on his face. When he looked up again, the gunman had vanished into the woods.

It was five or ten minutes more before Frank could stand. Legs shaking, he went to Targan. "Jake," he said. "Jake, what did he do to you?"

Targan lay on his back, testing each of his limbs. He worked his skis free and bent each leg slowly. He then flexed each arm gingerly.

He winced when he moved his right arm. "I think I'm okay," he said finally.

"It looked like he was trying to break your arm," Frank said. He helped Targan up onto his skis.

"It's not broken, I don't think," Targan said. He rotated the arm. "Bruised badly, but not broken."

"That's lucky," Frank said.

Targan managed a slight smile. "I drank a lot of milk as a kid. Strong bones, you know."

They put on their skis and found the trail again. "That was crazy," Targan said. "First he shoots at us, then he tries to shatter my arm."

"I figure he was after you," Frank said. "He wanted you out of judo for a while."

"Think it was Frierson?" Jake asked.

"Or Moubray, for some reason," Frank said. "He was supposed to meet us here, remember?"

They skied slowly, regaining their strength and keeping an eye out for the gunman.

"Hey, ski tracks," Frank said. He glided to a stop.

"Moubray?" Targan asked. "He was here on this trail before us?"

Frank nodded. They skied slowly, following the two ruts. Then Frank stopped again.

"Uh-oh," he said.

"What?" Targan asked. "The guy with the gun, do you see him?"

"No," Frank said. "He's not back. There, on the ground next to the tracks."

The two teens knelt down. A trail of red spots ran along the ski tracks. Frank touched one with his finger.

"Blood," he said.

12 False Confession?

Frank and Jake followed the trail for fifty yards or so.

"There!" Targan shouted. "Over there in the woods."

Frank saw someone lying on his side in the snow. "It's William," he said. "Come on."

They chucked their skis and picked their way between tree branches to get to Moubray.

"He's unconscious," Targan said.

Frank carefully lifted William's head. A nasty cut creased his temple. Two trickles of blood ran down his face.

"He's been shot," Frank said. "But the bullet only grazed him."

"Will he be okay?"

Frank plucked Targan's stocking cap off and placed it on William's head to cover the cut. "I think so. He needs a hospital, though."

"There's an emergency phone at the trailhead," Targan said. "I'll go." He ran back to the trail to put on his skis and go for help.

"Be careful," Frank shouted as Targan pumped down the trail. "That guy could still be out here."

Frank sat in the snow, cradling William's head. He listened to the wind bending the creaking pine limbs. Particles of icy snow dusted them. What Frank did not want to hear was a rifle shot. Targan had to make it to the phone.

Moubray's eyes fluttered open. "Frank," he said hoarsely. "Where am I?"

"In the park," Frank said. "We were going to go cross-country skiing, remember?"

William nodded almost imperceptibly, then shook his head, "No." His eyes closed in pain. "Feels like rockets are going off in my skull."

"You got shot," Frank said. "Stay cool. Jake went for help."

"Somebody called me this morning," William whispered. "I brought something here . . . or I was supposed to meet someone. I can't get it clear in my mind."

"Stay quiet," Frank said. "Help will be here soon."

It took about fifteen more minutes, but very quickly it became clear that Jake had made it to the phone.

The thumping rotors of a helicopter came first, followed by the high buzz of a snowmobile engine.

Careful not to blast them with his wind and the snow, the chopper pilot dipped close to the treetops nearby. Frank waved. The chopper rose and pulled off to a safe distance, hovering.

Then the snowmobile blasted through the trees, dragging a rescue litter on skids.

The driver shut the engine down and jumped off.

"Where'd you come from?" Frank asked.

"The ski lodge, dude," the driver said. His long blond hair hung out around his helmet. "How bad is it?"

"Can't tell," Frank replied. "He's in and out of consciousness."

Frank helped the ski patrol guy wrap a blanket around William and load him on the litter. He then climbed on the back of the snowmobile.

Frank tapped the guy's shoulder, letting him know he was ready to go. He hefted the rifle he'd borrowed from William but left his skis. He'd have to hope they were still there later.

An ambulance and the police waited for them in

the parking lot, along with Jake. As they loaded William into the rescue-squad van, Frank dug around in William's coat pocket for his keys. If William was going to be in the hospital for a while, he'd need some supplies from his room.

The ambulance pulled away, leaving one paramedic behind. She made Frank and Jake sit on the bumper of a police cruiser while she checked their injuries.

"Inhale," she said to Frank.

He took a deep breath and held it.

"Well, I don't think you have any broken ribs," she said. "Call your doctor, though, okay?"

Frank agreed.

While the medic checked out Jake's arm, Frank talked to the police.

"Everything happened so fast," he said. "Pretty much all I can tell you is that the guy was tall and had a long coat on. And he has a serious grudge against Jake over there."

The officers took notes, then let Frank and Jake go.

Frank drove Jake back to the athlete's dorm.

"This is the first time cross-country skiing has made me feel like I've just been through a three-day judo tournament," Jake said. "Man, am I sore."

"No kidding," Frank said.

"I'd like to get my hands on that guy without that hunting rifle," Jake said. "I'd twist his head right off his skinny neck."

"You'd have to wait your turn," Frank said. "And there wouldn't be much left when I was done."

In the dorm, Jake headed to his room to rest while Frank went to replace William's air rifle and pick up some stuff for his hospital stay.

He unlocked the door and went inside. Everything looked normal. Placing the gun on the bed, Frank pulled some clothes from a chest of drawers and wrapped a bath towel around William's toothbrush.

As he was about to leave, he decided he should put the gun back in the case against the wall. He propped the gun in the corner of the cabinet and covered it with the oil cloth.

Something didn't seem right, though. The cabinet looked empty. "What's missing?" Frank said to himself. Then it came to him. The crossbow was gone.

Who had it? Frank hadn't seen it close to Moubray in the woods. He picked up the clothes and left, locking the door behind him.

Frank sped to the hospital. It was a boxy concrete building with a long awning extending out over the main entrance walkway.

Frank jogged in and asked the man at the information desk about William.

The man tapped away at a computer. "He's been checked in. Room Four Sixteen."

"Can I go up and see him?"

"Not yet. He's getting a CT scan on his head. I expect he'll be in his room in an hour or so."

"Thanks." Frank took the elevator up to the fourth floor. After giving the bundle of clothes to a nurse outside William's room, he went to Joe's floor.

When he rounded the hall to Joe's room, he spotted not one but three officers standing outside the door. One was drinking a cup of coffee. Another was spinning a set of handcuffs around on his finger the way a lifeguard would spin a whistle lanyard.

Frank walked faster. Had there been another attack? Getting close to Joe's room, he heard voices coming from inside. He recognized Joe's—that was a relief. Who else was in there?

It was Allen Frierson. He stood by the window at the far side of the room. The first thing Frank noticed was that the right side of Allen's face was swollen. His right eye was purple around the lid.

"Frank," Joe said. "I was getting ready to check out and look who showed up."

Frank pointed at Frierson's black eye. "It was you, wasn't it? The guy in the mask who came after me in my van last night. That eye, it's from the ax kick I connected with."

Frierson looked worried and tired. "Yes. It was me." He rubbed at his swollen cheek self-consciously. "You almost knocked me cold."

Joe stood with arms crossed. "Tell Frank what you told me, Allen."

Allen found the wooden chair next to the window and sat down. "I did the stuff at the training center, not Victoria."

"You mean the rope and Iola getting shocked?"

Frierson nodded mournfully. "It was all Coach Sokal's idea," he said. "He couldn't believe the Olympic Committee didn't pick him to direct the new training center. For him, it was the opportunity of a lifetime."

"So he hated the fact that Montreux got it," Frank said.

Frierson nodded. "Sokal thought it was going to be his chance to make judo a hot spectator sport, just like football or basketball."

"Tell Frank how you got involved," Joe said.

"Sokal promised me a place on the junior team if I would help him," Allen said.

Frank remembered the file on Frierson in Sokal's

office. No wonder Sokal hadn't cut Allen from the team before the combat center opened. He wanted to use the kid.

"With my dad breathing down my neck all the time," Allen said, "I didn't feel as though I had a choice." He paused, rubbed his hands over his face, then continued.

"I rigged the fencing equipment and the rope. Then, with Sokal's help, I hid the electronics and the metal file in Victoria's office."

"How did you know how to sabotage the fencing gear?" Frank asked.

"My dad's an electrician, remember?" Allen said. "I've known how to do that kind of stuff since I was a kid."

"And sharpening Victoria's fencing swords?" Frank asked.

Allen raised his hand. "That was me, too. Sokal figured the next time she practiced she might hurt someone, get into trouble, and make Montreux look even more incompetent. We had no idea Joe would get stabbed, but it worked out perfectly."

"Yeah," Joe said. "A perfect visit to the hospital for me."

"Sorry," Allen mumbled. "I really, truly am sorry."

"What about the arrows?" Frank asked. "Who tried to plug me on the outdoor range?"

"That was Sokal," Allen said. "He's so in love with William Tell he couldn't resist putting that Milli Le Walt note on the arrow shaft as a sick joke."

"It all worked," Frank said. "Montreux got fired. Sokal got hired. But why jump me last night? Why the attacks on Jake Targan?"

"And who fed me a pillow snack?" Joe asked, still angry from his narrow escape.

"Last night was supposed to be only a warning, Frank," Allen said. "I didn't want it to turn into a full-blown fight. You were still asking questions. We wanted you to let Victoria take the fall and then let it drop."

Frank recalled that Allen had run from the van rather than fight. That fit with Frierson's story. "And Targan? What was with the hotplate and the wild stuff in the woods this morning?"

Allen's jaw dropped. "This morning?"

Allen and Joe obviously hadn't heard about the gunman yet. Frank filled them in.

Frierson went pale. "See that's just it," he said. "That's why I came here to confess to Joe."

"How do you mean?" Joe said.

"Once Sokal was named director, we stopped doing bad stuff," Allen said. "I have no idea who attacked Joe or who shot at you or who fixed Jake's hotplate to blow."

"Which means—" Frank started.

"That someone's still out there targeting people," Allen said, finishing Frank's thought. "Either Sokal's gone completely crazy and doesn't know when to stop, or some guy we don't know about has started doing even more scary stuff."

13 Crossbow Kidnapping

"Scary is right," Frank said. "William Moubray's lucky to be alive."

"Go outside, Allen," Joe said. "Say hello to those cops while I talk to my brother."

Head hanging, Frierson obeyed.

Frank shut the door behind him. "What do you think?"

Joe cracked his knuckles. "I don't know if he's telling the truth."

"It all makes sense," Frank said.

"Frierson's the person who benefits the most if Targan can't compete anymore," Joe said. "He steps into that weight class."

"That's true," Frank admitted.

"Allen didn't get here until about ten minutes before you," Joe noted. "He had plenty of time to chase you around the woods, then get over here. Maybe he injured Targan, shot Moubray, then got nervous and hurried over here to confess to smaller crimes, hoping he'd get away with it."

"No," Frank said. "The guy with the gun was taller than Allen. Only an inch or so, but taller."

"You were being shot at, Frank. Are you positive?" Frank hesitated.

"See," Joe said. "You just answered my question."

"We can still use Frierson," Frank said. "We take him to the training center with us and confront Sokal. See what he says when he finds out Frierson's singing like a bird."

Joe nodded. "Sounds like a plan."

It was afternoon when Frank pulled the van into the Combat Sports Training Facility parking lot. Joe sat in the passenger seat, while Allen sat quietly in the back of the van.

"The lot's almost full," Frank said. "Coach Sokal must be happy the place is so crowded on the first official day of his rule."

Allen didn't say anything.

"Here's your chance," Joe said to Allen as they all

got out. "You let Sokal know you're coming clean, confessing to all the things you did. We'll see how he reacts."

"What if he goes off?" Allen asked. "I mean . . . if the nut's crazy enough to shoot at people, who knows what he'll do."

"There's too much going on today," Frank said. "He won't try anything here."

Inside, it was obvious that all the coaches and athletes had been ordered to be especially helpful and happy.

A young woman greeted them as they walked onto the gym floor. She was handing out color pamphlets describing the training center and the parts of it that were open to the public.

Joe held up his hand. "Got one already, thanks."

Young kids, laughing and yelling, were getting a lesson on how to hold a foil properly. A judo blue belt tossed a medicine ball to her father. Music boomed from speakers as an instructor led a crowded aerobics class based on fencing and judo moves.

"At least the rope's been fixed," Allen said.

"You're right," Frank replied. "Too bad no one seems to feel like climbing it."

"Who are those guys who look like they're having no fun?" Joe asked. He gestured toward the solemn young men in training center sweatshirts standing next to each door.

"Off-duty cops, I bet," Frank said. "Looks like Sokal hired some professional security for the place."

Geneve Montreux, dressed casually in a black warm-up suit, strode over to the Hardys. She looked relaxed for the first time Frank could remember.

She smiled at the boys. "Joe," she said. "How are you feeling?"

"I'm fine, Ms. Montreux," Joe said. "I'm sorry you had to give up your position to Coach Sokal."

"Why, thank you," Montreux said. "It is sad, I suppose. But I'm enjoying coaching these kids today. It's been a while since I felt that way."

"We were actually looking for Coach Sokal," Joe said. "Is he here?"

Montreux shook her head. "I haven't seen him since this morning. Check around, though. I'm sure he's here somewhere." Montreux said goodbye and returned to her young students.

"Time to split up," Joe said.

"Sounds good," Frank replied. "You check Sokal's office. Allen and I will head downstairs."

Joe started to walk off. Frank grabbed his shoulder. "And, Joe," he said, "if you find him, please don't confront him. Come get us to back you up."

"You got it," Joe replied. "You do the same."

133

Joe nodded at the police officer guard as he passed through the double doors leading to the long hallway outside the gym. "Going to the bathroom, okay?" he said.

The officer raised an eyebrow. "I'll expect a full report when you get back."

"Funny."

The hallway was empty. Glancing over his shoulder, Joe made a beeline for the offices down the way.

Victoria's office still had yellow crime-scene tape across the door. He peeked in. It looked exactly as it had the day before.

The next door over had been Sokal's, but someone had already pulled the name tag from the door. Only a film of adhesive remained. Joe guessed Sokal had started to move into Montreux's director's digs.

Joe turned to Montreux's door. Her nameplate was gone as well. He knocked. "Coach Sokal, you in there?"

No reply.

Joe knocked again, then returned to Sokal's original office. He tried the door. To his surprise, it opened.

He peered in—no one. Stepping in, he turned on the light. What he saw surprised him even more.

Sokal's office had been messy the day before when Joe and Frank had broken in. It had been nothing like this, though.

If Sokal was switching offices, Joe would have expected some disarray. This was not disarray. The room looked as though a bomb had gone off.

The heavy steel filing cabinet had been toppled. Files lay open and strewn across the floor. The desk chair was on its back. A fist-size dent marred the new Sheetrock on one wall.

"Whooee!" Joe said. "There was some kind of major fight in here."

Frank and Allen descended the stairs to explore the basement. Strangely, all the lights were off as they passed through the fire doors and onto hard composite flooring.

Allen found the switches on the wall and flicked them on. The fluorescent bulbs shimmered pale green, then popped all the way on. A gentle hum filled the vast space.

"No one's here," Allen said.

"We've got to check," Frank said. "Don't back out now."

They moved to their right, toward the long indoor archery range.

"Empty," Frank said. "We should check all those storage rooms over there."

They crossed under the gymnasium floor. Over their heads, they heard the thumping of people jumping, falling, kicking.

At the opposite end of the basement, another long hallway, similar to the archery range, led away from the main floor. It was lined with unmarked white doors. Future locker rooms, offices, equipment rooms, Frank figured.

Allen entered the hallway first. He stayed close to the left-side wall, moving slowly.

Frank turned the knob on the first door. "It's open," he whispered to Allen.

Looking in, he saw only stacks of ladders, industrial-size drums of white paint, and other construction supplies.

"He's not down here," Allen said. "What would he be doing here?"

As they stepped back out into the hall, Allen froze. Frank almost bumped him, then saw what frightened Frierson.

A man dressed in full archery gear—mesh mask, vest, gloves, pants—faced them from the center of the hall.

He didn't have a sword, but he was carrying William Moubray's crossbow.

"Oh, no!" Allen said.

The man strode forward and pushed Frierson aside with his forearm. Allen stumbled to the side, eyes round with fear.

The man pointed the crossbow at Frank. He said nothing.

Squinting, Frank tried to see through the mesh face mask but couldn't identify the man.

The man said something, but Frank couldn't understand him. The mask, or perhaps a cloth over his mouth, muffled the man's voice. It sounded eerie, far away, ghostlike.

"Get down on the ground!" the man said, louder this time.

Allen dropped.

Frank had already faced this freak once today. He'd had enough. With a burst of strength, he jumped, kicking at the crossbow.

Frank's foot connected. The crossbow fired, sending the fierce bolt rocketing into the wall.

Frierson ran for it.

"Allen!" Frank shouted, but Frierson was long gone.

Frank's attacker ran farther down the hall. Frank took off after him.

He was gaining when the guy suddenly stopped and wheeled to face him. Somehow the guy had another bolt loaded. He leveled the bow at Frank's chest.

"Stop!" the guy shouted. "I won't miss this time!"

Frank stopped in his tracks. He'd gotten away with taking a chance once, but two times was one too many.

"Keep your hands high!" the voice behind the mask said. "And come with me."

Frank followed the guy to the end of the hall. There, the man opened a door and ushered Frank through it with the razor-sharp tip of the loaded bolt.

"Inside. Get on the ground next to your friend there!"

It took a few seconds for Frank's eyes to adjust to the dim light. The room was filled with folded judo mats and cork archery targets.

Sitting in a corner, hands tied and mouth taped, was Coach Sokal. His eyes searched Frank's for some sign of hope.

Frank had none to give.

"Get down!" the attacker shouted. "Sit down or I'll shoot you both!"

14 The Final Fall

Joe closed Sokal's office door as he left. He wondered whom he should tell first. Should he go straight to the cops guarding the training center, or should he go find Frank and Allen? He didn't have proof of anything yet. It just looked as if there had been some kind of struggle, as if someone had been after some files or after Coach Sokal, or both.

Joe headed back to the gym. As he passed a crowd of people waiting to try out the cross-country ski machines, Allen Frierson came sprinting up to him.

"Joe! Downstairs . . ."

"Spit it out!" Joe yelled.

"A guy with a loaded crossbow. He's got Frank!"

Joe led the way, taking the stairs two at a time. He stopped at the fire doors. Frierson hadn't kept up. Joe still didn't trust the guy and wondered if this might be a setup.

"Allen!" he whispered

"Right here," Frierson said. He came down the stairs more slowly. "I don't know if I'm up for this," he said. "Maybe we should get the police."

"Go ahead then, get them," Joe said. "I'm going after my brother."

Allen told Joe about the hallway where they'd run into the guy with the crossbow, then sprinted up the stairs.

Joe entered the basement. He crossed the cold floor quickly. All the doors along the hallway were closed. He padded along, listening at each door.

A few yards in, muffled voices reached him. He ran down to the door they came from.

"You made me a promise!" he heard a man scream. "You break that promise, and I'll make you pay for it!"

Joe recognized Frank's voice. "We can work this out. Let us go and we'll all talk about it."

"There's no time for that! It's over for you, Sokal. I'll close this whole place down for good if I have to."

Joe crossed the hall and opened the doors of one storage room after another. He found one with a wire equipment cage. Fencing vests and masks hung from hooks on the ceiling. Someone, the guy who had Frank, Joe guessed, had broken the lock.

Quickly Joe went in and grabbed a protective vest and a mask. Digging through a wooden crate, he found a nice gleaming saber. It was brand-new, and the grips weren't taped yet. It had the protective button on the end. Still, Joe figured, it was better than nothing.

He ran across the hall, listening for voices. All he heard was Allen Frierson, followed by three security guards, bashing through the fire doors at the other end of the room.

"Who's out there?" a voice from inside the room screamed.

Joe held up his hand, freezing Frierson and the security guards where they stood.

"I'm coming out!" the voice shouted. "If I see cops out there, I'm going to shoot Coach Sokal. You hear me?"

Joe kept quiet. He stepped away from the door and pressed himself as flat against the wall as he could.

The door opened a crack.

Joe knew this might be his only chance. He kicked the door with all his strength.

The guy staggered back. Holding the crossbow in one hand, he pointed it at Joe and fired.

Joe felt his blood run cold. The bolt zipped between his legs, tearing a two-inch rip in his jeans.

Too stunned to react, Joe allowed the fencer to rush past him into the hall.

When he turned, the guy had tossed the empty crossbow aside. Joe darted into the storage room, returning with his own saber.

"Now we've got a fair fight," Joe said. He turned his body sideways to present a smaller target and held out the saber at the ready.

Thinking quickly, Frank ripped the tape from Sokal's mouth. He struggled with the knotted ropes on the coach's wrists. He had to get out there to help Joe.

As the last strand of rope fell to the floor, Frank watched Joe and his opponent pass across the doorway, heading out to the open basement floor. He could hear the heavy steel blades bashing against each other.

Joe could tell his opponent was no fencer. The man was awkward with the sword. He was strong, though, and quick. And while the fencing mask hid the guy's face, Joe knew his expression was of crazed anger. He wanted to hurt Joe. That much was clear.

Once out in the main area, they had room to move. They circled each other, sometimes using circular columns or stacks of Sheetrock to avoid the whistling blows of the blades.

Joe feinted high. When his opponent lifted his saber to block, Joe slashed his blade down, slapping it across the man's knee.

"Rrraahh!" The guy let out a scream of pain. His legs almost buckled, but he recovered. Joe had to back off.

Out of the corner of his eye, Joe spotted Allen and the officers next to the fire doors. They stood apprehensively, wanting to jump in and help but not finding an opening.

Joe worked to back the other guy toward the cops. He hoped they could get the drop on him.

The fencer was too smart, though. He sensed Joe's plan and ran back to the center of the room.

Joe gave chase. Running, he stepped on a stack of Sheetrock. He'd hoped to use it to launch himself onto his opponent.

His foot slipped on some dust.

Joe fell. He lay sprawled half on the drywall, half hanging, head down toward the floor. He was defenseless. He had to get up, now!

Frank's heart sank. He saw his brother fall.

The other fencer had an opening. He lifted the

saber over his head, prepared to bring it down on Joe's exposed neck.

"No!" Frank yelled.

Joe rolled.

The saber blade sank into the drywall and stuck there.

Joe cracked his blade into the back of his attacker's knees. This time the guy dropped to the floor without a whimper.

Frank and the security guards were on the guy in seconds. They cuffed his hands behind his back and sent his weapon clattering far across the floor.

Joe stood up and pushed his mask back on his head. "Turn him over," he said. "Let's see who this joker is."

Frank roughly pulled off the fencing mask.

Allen Frierson gasped. "Dad!" he said.

"Sokal promised to put you on the team!" Mr. Frierson shouted. "I had to do something."

"You did something, all right," Joe said. "You got yourself arrested for kidnapping and attempted murder."

A few days later Frank, Joe, Callie, and Iola met Geneve Montreux and Victoria Huntington at the front door of the training facility. Joe had a backpack slung over his shoulder.

"I'm happy you could all come by," Geneve said.

"No. Thank you," Callie said. "A private fencing lesson from two of the best fencers in the world? This is awesome!"

Montreux smiled. "I used to be one of the best fencers in the world. Now it's Victoria's turn."

Victoria blushed.

They all walked across the empty gym floor to the fencing area. "So the two of you have made up?" Joe asked.

"Yes," Geneve said. "Victoria's back on the team."

"With a whole new attitude," Victoria said.

Victoria helped Callie and Iola get into vests and hooked up to the scoring lights. "I promise, no shocking experience this time."

"Thank goodness," Iola said.

"I can't believe Coach Sokal wanted my job so desperately," Montreux said.

"He took advantage of Allen Frierson to help him," Frank said.

"No one was supposed to get seriously hurt," Joe said. "But that stunt with the rope was almost a disaster."

"It was Frierson's father who really lost it, right?" Victoria said.

Frank nodded. "Allen did everything Sokal asked him to. When Sokal still said he was cutting him from the team, Mr. Frierson went ballistic. He modified

Jake Targan's hotplate to explode and tried to suffocate Joe."

"When that didn't work," Joe said, "he decided to hunt Jake down on the ski trails."

"He's going to spend a long time in prison," Frank said.

"What's going to happen to Sokal and Frierson?" Iola asked. She tested her foil by cutting a Z in the air.

"Sokal's banned for life from coaching," Montreux said.

"Police are going easy on Allen because he turned himself in," Frank said.

Victoria showed Callie how to move forward and back on the fencing strip quickly. "Are we ready to hook up to the lights?" she asked brightly.

"Yes!" Callie and Iola said simultaneously.

The two girls stood facing each other on the fencing strip.

Victoria walked to the scorer's table. She bent down and plugged the cord into the transformer.

"Yow!" Iola went stiff and collapsed on the ground.

Joe ran to her. He pulled the mask from her face.

"Just kidding!" she cried.

Everyone laughed.

"You got me," Joe said. "You got me good that time."

He helped Iola up, and the two girls began fencing.

Just then the front door slammed.

Frank and Joe turned to see Jake Targan walking across the gym. He came up and shook hands. "I just came from the hospital," he said. "William's getting out this afternoon."

"Great!" Frank said. "We'll have to help him get his stuff back to the dorm."

"Sounds good," Joe said. "What are you up to this morning, Jake?"

Targan reached in his duffel bag and tossed a judo jacket to Joe. "I thought we'd go a couple of falls," he said.

"Forget it," Joe said, laughing. "I brought my own fun." He zipped open his backpack and pulled out a football. "Let's toss this around. It's more my speed."

Split-second suspense...
Brain-teasing puzzles...

No case is too tough for the world's greatest teen detective!

MYSTERY STORIES
By Carolyn Keene

Join Nancy and her friends in
thrilling stories of adventure and intrigue

Look for brand-new mysteries
wherever books are sold

Available from Minstrel® Books
Published by Pocket Books

2313

**Do your younger brothers and sisters
want to read books like yours?**

**Let them know there
are books just for *them!***

They can join Nancy Drew and her best
friends as they collect clues and solve
mysteries in

THE

NANCY DREW

NOTEBOOKS®

Starting with

#1 The Slumber Party Secret

#2 The Lost Locket

#3 The Secret Santa

#4 Bad Day for Ballet

AND

**Meet up with suspense and mystery
in The Hardy Boys® are: The Clues Brothers™**

Starting with

#1 The Gross Ghost Mystery

#2 The Karate Clue

#3 First Day, Worst Day

#4 Jump Shot Detectives

 A MINSTREL® BOOK

Published by Pocket Books

2324

**The Fascinating Story of
One of the World's Most
Celebrated Naturalists**

Celebrating
40 years
with the
wild
chimpanzees

MY LIFE *with the*
CHIMPANZEES

by JANE
GOODALL

From the time she was girl, Jane Goodall dreamed
of a life spent working with animals. Finally, when she
was twenty-six years old, she ventured into the forests
of Africa to observe chimpanzees in the wild. On her
expeditions she braved the dangers of the jungle
and survived encounters with leopards and lions
in the African bush. And she got to know an amazing
group of wild chimpanzees—intelligent animals whose
lives bear a surprising resemblance to our own.

Illustrated with photographs

A Byron Preiss Visual Publications, Inc. Book

**A Minstrel® Book
Published by Pocket Books**

2403

BILL WALLACE

Award-winning author Bill Wallace brings you fun-filled
stories of animals full of humor and exciting adventures.

**BEAUTY
RED DOG
TRAPPED IN DEATH CAVE
A DOG CALLED KITTY
DANGER ON PANTHER PEAK
SNOT STEW
FERRET IN THE BEDROOM, LIZARDS IN THE
FRIDGE
DANGER IN QUICKSAND SWAMP
CHRISTMAS SPURS
TOTALLY DISGUSTING
BUFFALO GAL
NEVER SAY QUIT
BIGGEST KLUTZ IN FIFTH GRADE
BLACKWATER SWAMP
WATCHDOG AND THE COYOTES
TRUE FRIENDS
JOURNEY INTO TERROR
THE FINAL FREEDOM
THE BACKWARD BIRD DOG
UPCHUCK AND THE ROTTEN WILLY
UPCHUCK AND THE ROTTEN WILLY:
THE GREAT ESCAPE
THE FLYING FLEA, CALLIE, AND ME**

A MINSTREL® BOOK

Published by Pocket Books

648-28